A Conversation with a Cat

A Novel

Stephen Spotte

Published by Open Books

Copyright © 2018 by Stephen Spotte

Cover image © Atomic Roderick

ISBN-13: 978-1948598040

I've heard it said that cats talk to humans more than they talk to other cats, even in the wild, as an attempt to domesticate us.

D. W. Wilson, *Once You Break A Knuckle*

Foreword

After finishing this little novel all that remained was to devise a title, and one that perfectly describes the contents is *A Conversation with a Cat*. I immediately congratulated myself. Later came an uneasy feeling that it wasn't original, that someone had already used it. And then I remembered Hilaire Belloc's essay with the identical title, which was later included in a book of his essays published in 1931 and also titled *A Conversation with a Cat*. The volume was on my shelf. I blew the dust from its cover and read Belloc's brief essay again, concluding that his work had been misnamed, that it had not been a conversation at all; rather, it was Belloc musing "upon the necessary but tragic isolation of the human soul."

Belloc had been sitting in an English railway station drinking beer when a cat jumped onto his lap. Belloc expressed his lugubrious thoughts to her, addressing her as Amalthea after the nanny goat that had nursed the infant Zeus. The cat made no comment and soon hopped down to schmooze with another passenger in transit. Belloc's essay is actually an internal monologue. A mute cat contributes nothing to a conversation, and because Belloc had obviously not drunk enough beer to alter that situation I felt no guilt about recycling his title, in the process greatly improving its accuracy.

This is a work of fiction. I invented the narrative, although the recounting of my surgery and its subsequent effects on my mental state are true. Some of the material used to frame parts of the story set in the first century BCE (Before Current Era) is based on actual timelines and historical facts. For these I relied mainly on Stacy Schiff's splendid biography *Cleopatra: A Life*. For mood and a feeling of what life might have been like in Egypt then and earlier I absorbed Norman Mailer's magnificent novel *Ancient Evenings*. The nonfiction literature about cats contains much misinformation. For accurate descriptions of cat biology and behavior I used peer-reviewed findings from my treatise *Free-ranging Cats: Behavior, Ecology, Management*. Other salient sources of facts and inspiration included *The Life and Times of Cleopatra Queen of Egypt* by Arthur Weigall; Patricia Dale-Green's *The Cult of the Cat*; *The Cat and the Human Imagination* by Katharine M. Rogers; *Archy and Mehitabel* by Don Marquis; T. S. Eliot's *Old Possum's Book of Practical Cats*; Takashi Hiraide's *The Guest Cat*; Colette's *Le chat*; Sōseki Natsume's *I Am a Cat*, *Engineering in the Ancient World* by J. G. Landels; Robert Darnton's *The Great Cat Massacre and Other Episodes in French Cultural History*; and of course that extended nocturnal conversation on the outside deck with my own cat, Jinx.

1

The stories I'm about to tell recount a conversation I had recently with a cat, and so far as I can determine the content is true or mostly true. That is, some of it might be true. What the hell, I should be honest from the start and show my cards: I have no idea if what I'm about to say is the truth, meaning the entire tale could just as well be false. However in fairness to myself there are many different kinds of falsehoods the worst being the outright lie, which this surely is not. I was definitely present when events I'm about to describe took place, and Jinx was there too purring contentedly in the opposite deck chair, although not many people realize that cats also purr when they're anxious, leaving open the possibility he could have been messing with my head. Anyway certain events took place that I know really happened because I found evidence the next morning. For example I still sensed pain where a hot cigar ash had fallen on my bare scrotum during a particularly tense phase of our conversation, and the inside of my mouth felt as if I'd been licking ashtrays. The first is proof I smoked at least one cigar, the last sure evidence I smoked too many.

According to my dictionary a dialogue is a conversation between two people. As I said the conversation I'm about to present took place between a human and a domestic cat. I'm obviously the human because this is a first-person account of events as I recall them. Comparable first-cat accounts are regrettably rare because to my knowledge neither Jinx nor any member of his species has yet learned to type or pen its thoughts longhand.

Absent the writing part, which of course occurred after that special night, the dialogue itself was more confusing than you might imagine. I've associated with quite a few cats in my time but have never claimed to be Dr. Doolittle. None of them ever said anything to me in English, at least that I could hear. So the most obvious problem with having a conversation with a cat is being certain about what it's saying, if indeed it's saying anything at all and not merely making noises. In the experience I'm about to relate something extraordinary occurred, and what Jinx said popped into my head as a telepathic communication, not actual speech a person could hear and interpret. In other words to be sure I was actually hearing Jinx and not my brain talking to itself two conditions had to be met. First my mind had to be in a fragile state induced by disorientation and recent pain. Second I had to be really stoned.

Jinx lives with my wife Lucia and me. He resembles a miniature melanistic leopard with his pure black coat and big yellow eyes and his face like an Egyptian death mask that never changes expression. Even black leopards still retain their spots, although not being a leopard Jinx is simply black all over. And his eyes can be unnerving: pity, hope, despair, hunger. . .transmitted through his golden gaze they're the same, at least to us humans. That cats are often described as cruel is an impossibility, a human attribute unfairly placed on them. Cats of all species are predators, and an act of cruelty from the standpoint of human values is irrelevant in their case. Still, they have surprising depth of character and understanding, as Jinx proved to me.

Events leading to that night on my outside deck were nothing unusual. They could have happened to you or to anybody. The previous week I'd flown to Providence, Rhode Island and met up with the renowned marine artist Keith Reynolds for a few days of fishing in the Thousand Islands region of northern New York State on the Canadian border. Keith and I go back to the early 1970s when we both lived and worked in New York City. We make these fishing trips every couple of years when the urge hits and then one of us calls the other. Keith and his wife Sandra live in Bristol, Rhode Island not far from the airport. He picks me up and we drive in his car the six or so hours to Alexandria Bay on the St. Lawrence River, generally after tourist season in early September. There we check into a second-rate motel and prepare to fish the following day, which mostly involves unpacking our gear, arranging a boat rental, procuring a supply of junk food, and picking up a can of earthworms at the local bait shop. The worms generally last the ensuing week because our rooms have refrigerators. When worms are packaged in shredded wet newspaper they ordinarily survive several days in a wriggly state if kept cool.

The next morning after early breakfast we motor out into the St. Lawrence where we anchor and make inane wagers about the fishes we'll catch. This has to do mainly with size: I bet mine is bigger than yours, har, har. We peer over the gunwales and watch our quarry swim languidly through emerald forests of elodea, Eurasian milfoil, and other waterweeds bent over and undulating in the current sweeping east toward the Atlantic Ocean. Rocky islands, many less than an acre with a single summer house accessible only by boat, pop up all around like the gray backs of turtles, trees and shrubs clinging precariously to their steep sides. We spend the day waving to tour boats, occasionally bailing water from our decrepit craft, unhooking and releasing undersized perch, and shedding sweaters and jackets when at midday a little sunlight finally sneaks around the clouds. Actually catching a fish is secondary. To paraphrase George Orwell, fishing is the opposite of war. We sit there with our lines in the silent river reprising old stories, telling lewd jokes, recounting youthful conquests of maidens now surely crones but eternally lithe and fair in our memories, and about everything we lie.

During quiet intervals I might pencil a few notes while Keith studies our surroundings. He sees what I never have. As a scientist I would describe his paintings as masterly depictions of water's phase changes, magical scenes in which liquid hesitantly evaporates into mist, a metamorphosis he captures so subtly it's barely perceptible. In his created world of neither air nor water a translucent sail emerges suddenly from a fog bank or a rusty trawler seems to levitate under a weakened sky. After such a day of musings and good fellowship we return to the dock, stash the gear in our rooms, and venture into the town of Alex Bay to drink beer and eat greasy food. The next day is a repeat of the one before.

Occasional abdominal agony over the previous several weeks in response to greasy food should have tipped me off. At week's end Keith dropped me at an airport motel because the flight to Tampa left early the next morning. In the night I experienced excruciating abdominal pain. I made it onto the flight, but during the first night at home the pain returned with such fierce urgency that Lucia took me to the emergency room at Sarasota Memorial Hospital.

"Ruptured gall bladder," the admitting physician said while squinting at some transparencies he held up to the light. "Surgery first thing tomorrow morning."

I was checked into Room 335, the relevance of this location to be revealed a little later. My roomie said his

5

name was Jimbo, that I'd have to shout at him because he was mostly deaf. He told me he was ninety-three and that he was tired of getting out of bed every hour and dragging his I.V. cart, not to mention his ass, to the bathroom just to take a piss. I suggested he could piss in the plastic bottle put beside his bed for that purpose, but I don't think he heard me.

"Nice to meet you, Jimbo," I said.

"*What?*" he said.

A nurse hooked me up with an I.V. and soon I felt that warm surge of morphine. It was good, *really* good. The pain dissipated, or seemed to. Either way it made no difference. I wanted sleep but Jimbo had his TV cranked up to full volume. In my altered state I thought I could see the walls vibrating, paint peeling away in strips, Jimbo doing the hand-jive in his bed.

"*Hey, Jimbo!*" I yelled. "*How about turning down the volume!*"

"*What?*" Jimbo shouted back.

"*Can you turn down the fucking TV?*"

"Well, sure I can. You don't have to yell for chris-sakes. I'm not that deaf."

"Actually Jimbo, you are."

"*What'd you say? I told you I'm practically deaf and you need to yell at me.*"

"I just did."

"*What?*"

In the night they came and took Jimbo away somewhere. He didn't come back. They'd given me a plunger attached to that I.V. so I could balance the morphine with the level of pain. I pushed it at frequent intervals despite knowing it was equipped with a governor. I figured my thumb needed the exercise.

Next morning they wheeled me to surgery prep. I lay on a cot in an ante-room while a scrawny Jamaican with a gold front tooth shaved my abdomen using a disposable razor. He wore a Rasta tam to cover his dreadlocks and a surgeon's cap over that.

"Mon," he said, "you *do* got some angry belly fuzz. Woo-*eee*"

"Yep, it grows freely by the time you attain geezerhood," I said. "Wish it was on my head. I sure could use a stick of ganja about now, you know, maybe ease the anxiety. I'll even join your religion. Always loved Bob Marley and that Haile Selassie. Couple of okay dudes. By the way, I think I'm stoned."

He looked up at me slyly, gloved hands covered in shaving cream. "You ain't anxious, mon." He grinned. "You oughta see de people come troo dis place. Some we gotta strap to dey beds, dey be jumping off, we doan. Yeah, you stoned awright." He gave my I.V. bag a quick nod. "Now hold wit me, I gotta do aroun' dis belly button. Gall bladder surg'ry dey drill down troo dat ting, drill you a new hole." He thought that was funny as hell and paused to bend over and cackle like a demented hen.

Surgery was successful; that is, my gall bladder is no longer part of my anatomy. Because the fever recorded at check-in had not subsided, antibiotics were added to the I.V. stream. This proved a prescient decision considering that pre-surgery blood cultures later revealed sepsis. Not surprising, the surgeon told me during his rounds that afternoon. Evidently the gall bladder had actually exploded. I should have come to the E.R. sooner, he said. I told him there hadn't been time because I was fishing. It seemed a logical response considering Keith's dictum that if you're too busy to fish then you must be really busy. He didn't reply. He just turned and left still wearing his funny little surgeon's cap with some string ties dangling off it.

I was back in my room before noon. Lucia was waiting. We talked, but I knew I was mostly incoherent. I suddenly realized that although I was participating in what seemed like a rational conversation Lucia had left and gone home. In the night a squall blew in off the Gulf of Mexico. Wind gusts pounded the city and the sodium security lamps on the hospital roof as seen through the rain-streaked windows seemed to be melting, their lights dissolving into strange exotic shapes. It was then I heard the voice. I thought it must be a frantic stray cat trapped on the third-floor roof just outside, but the battering rain broke apart and muffled the noise. I kept hearing it off and on in the night through the morphine haze now augmented and thickened by oral oxycodone.

Then I realized it wasn't a cat screaming *meow* but a human voice emanating from the room above mine and oozing, it seemed, down through the concrete slab directly to my brain. It sounded—or rather felt—strangely clear and unimpeded as if a hearing aid had been mysteriously implanted in my inner ear. And that single catlike term wasn't all. When I listened carefully the voice of a woman apparently locked in the room above me was yelling, "*Let me out neeeow!*" Occasionally she became violent and started stamping her feet and shoving the furniture around, slamming objects into walls and shouting, "*Let me out neeeow!*

Duty nurses barged in and out through that first night and the several subsequent nights I was incarcerated. They switched on lights, stuck needles into my increasingly perforated flesh, forced thermometers under my tongue, took my pulse, and asked if I needed to take a leak. That first night during one such disruption of reveries I inquired about the lady upstairs.

"Oh her," the nurse sighed while slurping up another syringeful of blood and prospecting along my abdomen for post-surgery pain. "She's a sad case. The poor thing is mentally ill, but Florida doesn't have enough mental health facilities to accommodate every patient so she gets passed around to regular hospitals in the area. We have her now. When a bed opens at a psychiatric facility she'll be shipped there until someone in worse shape comes along, then we might get her back again or she'll go somewhere else, you never know."

The nurse told me all this with her lips in an odd half-smile, enigmatic like the Mona Lisa's. Such expressions are hard to interpret when you've recently downed another hit of oxycodone and even the sink and bedside table are smiling back. She left and closed the door, and the room was abruptly dark again except for pale remnants of yellow light from the roof outside. The squall passed through leaving only thin rain. The sodium lamps regained form and climbed back atop their posts. Echoes of the ruckus upstairs had subsided, the voice now stilled. A clock on the wall said two a.m. I pushed the plunger and doped out.

After several days I went home. Two nights later my temperature spiked and it was back to the hospital where X-rays revealed pneumonia, courtesy of the previous stay. Once again I was hooked up to the same I.V. combination as before. This time I was rolled into Room 435 directly above my old room. My door was closed and as the drugs kicked in I could hear only faint noises in the hall: laughter from the nurses' station, footsteps of occasional geriatric patients shuffling past rolling squeaky I.V. rigs, echoes of doors opening and shutting. The afternoon duty nurse appeared, and I asked him what had become of the crazy woman who occupied this room just a few days earlier. "What lady?" he said. This room had been empty nearly two weeks until I showed up.

My fever gradually attenuated, and according to a series of chest X-rays the shadow of pneumonia in the right lung was shrinking rapidly. A day or so later they sprung me. Back home I was making every effort to keep the hospital buzz going. My circulatory system was still ablaze with morphine and there was a bottle of oxycodone on standby in the other room. I'd retrieved a full jug of Venezuelan sipping rum from the liquor cabinet along with a snifter, and several pre-rolled doobies lay prone on the cocktail table. The sun had long since set, and Lucia had gone upstairs to get ready for bed and read after advising me to please not topple off the deck.

I'd just finished this monologue, although for whom I wasn't yet certain. I hoped Jinx had at least heard me. That was probably a given unless he was deep in slumber. After all, his eyes were closed. Hearing to a biologist is the reception of sound; listening is hearing with an element of interpretation and often anticipation. Was Jinx's auditory system participating in either? Without lifting his head from the deck chair or opening his eyes I heard him say, "Cats never really sleep so don't be fooled by our somnolent postures or lack of enthusiasm. We do dream, although not as you might define dreaming. Take a dog. When it sleeps it dreams of something mundane like chasing a rabbit or pissing on a tree or rolling on a dead fish. But sleeping cats revisit history complete with the sounds, sights, and smells as they were perceived in the moment."

He paused for a stretch and a yawn before continuing. "People mostly don't notice cats, but one is usually nearby. Any cat present at a momentous event records its experiences and sensations into living memory for benefit of all future cats for all time. One cat's memoir is the memoir of every cat who ever lived, their stories differing only in the details. Our history is yours too, the distinction being that ours is embedded, embodied, emboldened, and (I apologize in advance) embellished in a universal felid memory. And memory—don't ever forget—is fiction. Trust it at your peril.

"So there you are. Want a companion who hangs on your every word and gesture, whose immediate hope and desire is to lick your lips after having just licked his own balls and asshole? If you find that appealing get a dog. Dogs also satisfy the peculiar pride of ownership so necessary to insecure humans believing themselves inadequately loved and admired. If on the other hand you value scintillating conversation and are willing to set aside the drivel written down by fellow humans who label themselves historians—and if you wish to step directly back among the warts and festering sores of *real* history and don't object to it being told to you by a personage who truly doesn't give a rat's ass about your stupid emotions or personal problems—I offer this advice: befriend a cat, get stoned, kick back, and listen up. So. . .think you're ready to imbibe history from a cat's perspective?"

"Sure," I said.

"Let's start by telling me what you know about cat histories," said Jinx.

"Not much," I said. "I read Robert Darnton's *The Great Cat Massacre*, an event perpetrated in 1740 by a community of drunken apprentice printers and recorded by Nicolas Contat, who was one of them. They ran through the rue Saint-Séverin of

Paris slaughtering cats—pets and strays alike—for
no apparent reason other than hating their bourgeois
masters at least one of whom fed his pet cats 'roasted
fowl' while relegating the fare of his apprentices to
moldy leftovers and other disagreeable items. And
I know about Archy and Mehitabel from reading
Don Marquis' little books. Marquis was a journalist
working for the New York *Sun* in 1920s Manhattan.
He wrote a column called "Sun Dial" and it's there
we first hear of Archy and Mehitabel. Archy was the
more literary, but it was mainly Mehitabel's adven-
tures he recorded. You could say he was Boswell to
Mehitabel's Dr. Johnson.

"Archy was a cockroach, Mehitabel a scroungy
female alley cat. They were friends. She was skank from
nose to tail and partial to down-at-the-heels one-eyed
toms. She'd disappear for days and once even surfaced
in Paris, although how she managed that Archy never
said. Oh, and she detested motherhood. Couldn't wait
to wean her little bastards and split the scene.

"Marquis hadn't known of Archy's existence until
arriving early one morning at the *Sun*. Someone was
pecking away at his typewriter in the other room using
just one key at a time, leaving an interval of several
seconds between keystrokes as if typing laboriously
with a single index finger. When Marquis peeked
around the corner at his desk there was a cockroach—
an unusually large cockroach—climbing atop the
machine and diving headfirst onto a key. The impact
was hard enough to depress it fully and leave an ink

impression on the blank sheet of paper Marquis had absent-mindedly left in the roller the previous night. The roach repeated this process again and again.

"Fortunately for him Marquis' machine evidently had an automatic carriage return, although I don't think those were yet available back then. Anyway the roach finally finished whatever he was typing, wiped his brow with one of his six wrists (or what passes for a brow on a cockroach), jumped to the floor, and disappeared into a crack in the wall. Marquis walked quietly to his desk and sat down expecting to see a scatter of random characters. He was stunned to find a free-verse poem about a cat named Mehitabel and signed 'Archy' at the bottom of the page. Everything had been typed in lower-case characters, probably because Archy couldn't figure a way of striking the shift key and target key simultaneously during his dives. Thereafter Marquis left a sheet of blank paper in his machine every afternoon before departing the office along with enough sandwich crusts to see Archy through the night. By morning the poor thing had written another poem and must have had a helluva headache."

"Of course I know about Mehitabel," Jinx said. "Archy left behind a fine record of her history. But you seem to know it already so where is this going? Like what's the point of retelling it to me?"

"Mehitabel always claimed to be a reincarnation of Cleopatra," I said. "You know who I mean. . .*that* Cleopatra. Does this indicate I'm destined to return as Tony the Tiger from the cereal box or maybe Hobbes from the comic strip? I'd like to know so I can plan ahead. I have a family, remember?"

"Don't worry, dumbass. Cats don't return reincarnated as humans or other cats or as anything else. A dead cat is a dead cat, and dead humans are equally dead. Mehitabel was delusional. However Cleopatra—*the* Cleopatra—did have a cat. In fact she had three although only one took notes, so to speak, and we have her history on file. Quite a story if you'd like to hear it. A bit long and harrowing."

"I have all night," I said.

"Then take a hefty toke on that doobie," said Jinx, "and blow some smoke my way."

2

Maybe because the palace was besieged and there wasn't much else to do we noticed Mistress and General C knocking sandals atop the royal mattress more than usual. The three of us were usually in the room too, making it hard not to notice. Many times they were too quick to even turn down the pearl-encrusted bedspread threaded with gold and silver, an accessory putatively valued at one million sesterces by the Royal Keeper of Inventories.

Ordinarily they acted civilized and did it missionary-style on the silk sheets, but if in a hurry the general simply bent Mistress over the mattress, hiked up her tunic, and took her from behind like a tomcat. A few grunts and spasms, some grimacing and softly spoken niceties, and it was finished. Afterward they rolled over and rested a few moments before dressing, leaving the boudoir, and getting back to their jobs of ruling Egypt and Rome. The Mediterranean world was in chaos, Rome having just survived a civil war while Egypt, as a Roman protectorate, stood by nervously awaiting its fate now that General C had emerged the winner. In truth most of Rome was pissed at him for hanging out here in Alexandria toting up sack time with Mistress instead of taking care of business back home in the Senate.

Both Mistress and the general were workaholic multi-taskers by anyone's definition. At any hour either might be dictating memorandums to an amanuensis about grain shipments, inventories, taxation, or deployment of ships and troops throughout the known world while simultaneously watching a play in one of the palace's theaters or listening to an orchestra of royal lutists and harpists. Later there might be dignitaries to entertain, courtiers to humor, intrigues to assess, disputes to mediate, a beheading, strangling, or cryptic poisoning to arrange. The palace staff's only purpose was to serve them, and because they slept rarely so did everyone else. Any assistant, servant, slave, or military adjutant, regardless of status or rank, might be summoned at any moment of the day or night.

Mistress—Queen Cleopatra to you—had at this turbulent time developed a keen interest in poisons, hoping to discover one that worked quickly and painlessly in case she might need it to kill herself someday. Her newly acquired hobby involved experimenting on prisoners housed in the palace dungeon who were destined for execution anyway. Each week couriers arrived from the far corners of the Orient bearing new toxic formularies and live specimens of rare poisonous plants and venomous animals. She tested them all, observing their effects dispassionately while making note of convulsions and bouts of vomiting, assessing intervals between screams, and recording time to fatality. The subjects were doomed no matter the outcome: those who survived were humanely strangled by the guards.

At the moment Mistress and General C were focused on fending off the outraged populace of Alexandria, which had joined forces with a segment of the Roman army hoping to depose Mistress in favor of Ptolemy XIII, her younger brother, legal husband, and co-regent. Considering the circumstances, aside from regularly patrolling the palace defenses and checking off the items mentioned above, what was left except fucking? Following these frequent noonies royal seamstresses giggling silently behind their hands crept in from the hall to wipe away stains left on the bedspread and make any necessary repairs.

Who is speaking? I am. My name is Annipe, which means daughter of the Nile, and I'm a cat; rather, I was one in life. I've since been reduced to molecules and elements and diluted to near infinity in the Mediterranean Sea, although atoms of me have subsequently fallen in tears and rain, been flushed into sewers, and even decanted as wine into goblets. I'm everywhere although all that persists from the corporeal me is this tale, which occupies space only in your mind.

My littermates were Anubis (the afterlife) and Aten

(the disk of the sun). Our ancestors had been African wildcats from whom we inherited our tall stance, long legs and tails, and slender torsos. Anubis and I were black and shiny as pitch with eyes of molten gold. African wildcats are spotted like leopards and even in our melanistic form our spots were visible, black though they were, evidence that neither a leopard nor a wildcat can ever truly hide its spots, much less "change" them. Aten was albino, white as alabaster under the desert sun and bearing the pink nose and eyes of a newly opened rose. Every human who saw him looked twice in astonishment, and the uneducated occasionally genuflected as he passed by. Being color-blind, other cats were routinely unimpressed. To the rest of us he looked and behaved as any cat except for his snooty attitude and affectation to pose in the manner of actors, Roman senators, and royalty.

In fairness, Aten's unusual appearance got us that palace gig. Cats were sacred in ancient Egypt, represented by the cat goddess Bastet and worshipped at temples dedicated in her honor. Then along came this white cat with pink eyes. How could he not be a god incarnate? Even when an ordinary household cat died all human members of the family were required to shave their eyebrows as a sign of mourning, and when the head of a household passed away and was mummified his cat was killed and mummified too. Tradition also called for embalming a few mice so the cat would have snacks in the netherworld.

That cats were worshipped and temples dedicated

to our goddess is certainly no less than we deserve. And the citizens protected us with a fervor to make Bastet proud. I'll give an example. When Mistress was still a young girl a Roman official visiting Alexandria killed a cat accidently, whereupon a mob of enraged citizens attacked him and ripped him apart. Even earlier, in 525 BCE, the Persians led by the general Cambyses III invaded Egypt only to be stopped at the city of Pelusium. Cambyses ordered images of Bastet painted on the shields of his soldiers, at which point Egyptian resistance collapsed. Think of it: the Egyptians surrendered their country rather than see their cats disrespected. How many times has that happened in human history?

It should come as no surprise that we cats have always considered ancient Egypt the apex of human development and agree unanimously that after Egypt fell to Roman hands your species underwent a steady regression, a reverse cultural evolution. Romans were arrogant. They thought that anyone who didn't speak Latin was a barbarian, but to Alexandrians *they* were the barbarians. And through the centuries others followed. Want proof? Look around at the state of the world and don't blame us cats for what you see.

An albino and two melanistic kittens make an unusual threesome, especially with Mom being just an ordinary stray. And Dad? A litter of kittens can have multiple paternity and "dads" is more likely. Furthermore a tom doesn't hang around after mating, making for a wise kitten that knows its own father. Mom had been skulking about outside the royal kitchens living on rodents and the occasional scrap tossed her way by scullery slaves. We were born nearby among some garbage bins. No sooner did the kitchen slaves find us than the family was taken inside and allowed run of the pantries. Mom reared us to weaning, after which the slut vanished back into Alexandria's avenues and alleys. A handmaiden eventually showed us to Mistress and we became official residents of the palace, allowed to sleep in the royal bedroom.

This was about 51 BCE when Mistress was eighteen, a petite girl with piercing black eyes, an aquiline nose and strong chin, and the voice of an angel. She was still naïve and unsuspecting of her monumental place in history, although even as a young woman no one possessed a sharper, more cunning mind. Within that slender frame burned relentless ambition sufficient to turn the ancient world upside-down. For twenty-two years Mistress ruled Egypt with me beside her and in her heyday was the wealthiest person in the Mediterranean, flattered and the recipient of gifts from every sovereign needing funds to raise an army or navy for the purpose of conquering a nearby kingdom and murdering and enslaving its citizens. War was the providence of everyone in power, and armies and navies were expensive. Mistress was thus viewed as a potential bankroller by other rulers.

My brothers and I matured quickly from kittens into young adults pampered by Mistress and her slaves, in particular Iras, Mistress' hairdresser and

Charmion, her favorite handmaiden. These women were her own age having been born into slavery there in the palace, and both had served and entertained her since childhood. Mistress loved and trusted them more than her own sisters, especially that scheming bitch Anisoë. They were treated more as valued employees than slaves, recipients of cash bonuses and other gifts. Mistress often wore a tunic or some other article of clothing only once before giving it to Iras and Charmion to sell in the marketplace. Both were frugal with their gains and while still quite young could afford to buy slaves of their own, rendering the very concept of slavery not just redundant but perplexingly hierarchical.

We were taught as kittens to jump into a lidded basket woven of river reeds. Our basket was carried by a Nubian slave without a name, our personal needs attended by an ever-present handmaiden. No luxury was too excessive. We lapped fresh camel's milk from dishes of pure gold. Our collars, dyed royal purple, had been fashioned from the soft skins of peafowls. We shit in trays of hammered silver filled with sparkling white sand dug from the nearby beach at Necopolis.

General C—you no doubt remember him as Julius Caesar—was the most famous soldier of his day. He was also renowned for being chronically bankrupt. He once gave a pearl to a mistress valued at more than the annual salaries of twelve hundred Roman soldiers. General C was profligate in all ways imaginable, a collector of gems and manuscripts, of villas and horses and chariots and women. In addition to these hobbies was the expense of hiring, equipping, and deploying armies and navies for which he was always borrowing money. The recent civil war pitting his military forces against General Pompey's had cost him dearly, and he badly needed cash.

Mistress' father Ptolemy XII had ruled so ineffectively that the citizens of Alexandria exiled him to Rome. He stayed there eight years giving lavish parties, writing poetry and playing his lute, and running up enormous debts totaling some three thousand talents. General C's reason for visiting Egypt after the war was to collect Ptolemy XII's debts from his children so he could reimburse his own creditors. Although he was willing to be generous and forgive half the tab, he fully expected Mistress and Ptolemy XIII to cough up the rest. They could easily afford to but Mistress had another plan, which was dumping her brother and ruling Egypt alone with Rome's backing. This involved getting General C firmly in her camp. However Pompey remained an impediment. Immediately following the war Pompey hauled ass to Egypt to avoid capture by General C and on arrival he planned to request exile and beg funds from Mistress and her co-regent so he could eventually rebuild his forces. As events happened he never actually touched the African shore.

Ptolemy XIII, age thirteen and a sniveling little prick, had meanwhile connived to exile his sister to the Syrian desert. Being a city girl and accustomed to life's finery she showed no interest in living permanently in a tent among camel drivers and wearing dirty Bedouin garb. She fully intended to re-occupy the palace. We cats felt the same. The desert was just a gigantic sandbox and no place for the likes of us. Even a day without a cooling sea breeze, a soft pillow, a bowl of milk, and a comfortable place to shit was unthinkable. Luckily Mistress had been forced to leave in a hurry, and we were among her numerous possessions left behind in care of Iras and Charmion. I'll tell you shortly how Mistress maneuvered around Ptolemy XIII after his top advisers, knowing Pompey was on the way to Egypt, suggested that his ship be intercepted and Pompey beheaded as a way of sucking up to General C, also due to arrive any day. This was a fatal mistake, an object lesson against listening to bad advice especially when your brain trust includes a professor and a eunuch.

On arriving in Alexandria General C immediately ensconced himself in the palace with Ptolemy XIII's blessing, protected only by a small force of his own soldiers. Ptolemy XIII was the lone pharaoh on hand with Mistress exiled to the desert and thus the only host, and when he presented General C with Pompey's severed head and grinned stupidly expecting attaboys the general started to cry. Pompey had once been General C's son-in-law until political exigencies made divorce necessary, and beneath that weathered skin and cold stare beat the heart of a kind man. Pompey XIII had clearly screwed up because

General C was willing to forgive his former relative and colleague and spare his life. Now he was stuck arranging a funeral for just his severed head, the body once attached to it having been tossed overboard.

Knowing General C was now in Alexandria, Mistress' allies smuggled her through the Syrian and Egyptian deserts and into the palace. There the loyal Apollodorus the Sicilian stuffed her into a sort of duffle, slung her over his shoulder, and whisked her past Ptolemy XIII's guards directly to Caesar's private quarters. When a bewitching young woman sprang suddenly from a bag at his feet the general was first astonished, then charmed. Cleopatra was twenty-one, Caesar fifty-two, a classic May-December meeting featuring two of the ancient world's superstars.

History has Cleopatra being rolled into a carpet instead of hidden in a bag, but that isn't true. Nor did she go directly to General C's quarters. She was first taken to her boudoir where a hot bath was drawn. Then Iras did her hair and Charmion applied her makeup, and afterward they dressed her in a translucent white tunic. Are you serious? Do you really think a queen and a goddess would permit the ruler of Rome to see her pop out of a duffle straight from the desert disheveled and unwashed? Not a chance. I *know* what occurred. My brothers and I had just finished a bowl of warm milk when Mistress silently entered the royal bed chamber while Apollodorus the Sicilian assumed his post by the door. It wasn't easy getting Mistress into that bag afterward without mussing her hair, smearing her makeup, and ruining the lines of her tunic. Everyone knows how easily linen wrinkles. She fully counted on General C handling all that himself.

Despite his chastisement over the incident with Pompey's head Ptolemy XIII still worshipped General C as a father figure, his own father Ptolemy XII having been such a cowardly spendthrift, drunkard, middling lutist, and overall schmuck. Satisfied that Mistress was now dehydrating in the desert among the rocks and lizards, drinking from polluted wells and living on camel jerky, he was dumbstruck by what he saw on being summoned to General C's palace quarters. There was his sister and wife lounging on a couch and smiling a foxy smile while stroking something standing proudly erect and saluting underneath the general's toga. Enraged and feeling betrayed he ran outside weeping and rallying the populace which, as history accurately tells us, responded enthusiastically.

Out in the streets Ptolemy XIII convinced the citizens of Alexandria that Mistress—not he—was the usurper when in truth that shoe fit both. With the Alexandrians backing him Ptolemy XIII's troops besieged the palace intent on starving Mistress and General C into submission, a situation they dealt with by spending even more time grappling on the mattress. Poor Charmion found herself changing the sheets several times a day and calling in the royal seamstresses at all hours. Even cats understand how sex can be a terrific attitude adjuster by relaxing the muscles, releasing endorphins, and quelling jumpy nerves. There's nothing like a quickie when you're under a genuine siege while a sword almost literally hangs over your head.

General C's outnumbered guards fought bravely. Wealthy citizens declining to participate against them in person armed their slaves instead. Trailed by other slaves lugging picnic baskets and amphorae of wine they took up stations on ridges and atop buildings to watch the battles. Slaughter is always a wonderful spectacle. My brothers and I had a perfect view from high on a window ledge outside the boudoir until smoke from the fires drove us inside. To keep Ptolemy XIII's forces and his Roman allies from hijacking Egypt's warships, General C ordered them burned. The conflagration consumed most of the harbor including part of Alexandria's famed library with its one-hundred-thousand scrolls. Fires in the vicinity of the harbor crackled for days, their smoke blocking out the sun. Just when the situation seemed most dire the general's reinforcements arrived, and he emerged victorious.

General C's officers had often been critical of his generosity with defeated enemies, and in hindsight he probably should have chopped off Ptolemy XIII's head upon being presented with Pompey's. Events nonetheless worked in his favor and that of Mistress. Ptolemy XIII was a spoiled adolescent, not a soldier, and his final mistake was leading his own military against General C's. He drowned in the Nile trying to escape the battle, and Mistress was rid of a pesky sibling without the need of resorting to poison. We cats never liked him anyway. He presented more as a dog person with his halitosis and obsequious manner. The only remnant of Ptolemy XIII ever recovered was his golden armor. It's puzzling to me why anyone would wear armor when faced with the imminent prospect of swimming. Then again as a cat I would never do something so stupid as jump into a river.

This was 47 BCE when General C eventually quit dawdling in Alexandria and returned to Rome leaving Mistress knocked up. She gave birth to a son the next year and named him Caesarian, or "little Caesar," a diminutive associated in later millenniums with a chain of pizzerias. Meanwhile the general was holding a triumph to celebrate his victories, and among the spoils of the Alexandrian scuffle he paraded through the streets were Ptolemy XIII's armor and Mistress' little sister Arsenoë shackled behind a cart. As a prisoner of war her future was not promising.

General C's ego had become greatly swollen during Mistress' pregnancy, although considered in isolation this event was doubtfully responsible especially because both Mistress and he were married to other people, a situation reducing Caesarian to nothing more than a little bastard. Throughout his career the general had scattered his wild oats like any effective tomcat and at no time prayed for crop failure. Having fathered progeny across the known world one more scarcely mattered, except that in this case his son's mother was sufficiently rich to outfit armies and navies of whatever size a great leader and demigod might require to reinforce his authority and expand Rome's borders. Add to that the fact that Caesarian was his only son, or at least the only one he recognized.

Alexander had been the most famous soldier in the ancient world; General C ranked second, and he didn't like it. General C's self-esteem had always been out-sized, sufficient to make eyes roll when he pontificated before the Roman Senate, but in those post-Alex-andria days he was practically a caricature. For the first time in his life he began a regimen of personal beautification, splashing himself with sweetly scented ointments, arranging his thinning hair in a comb-over, dressing in royal purple togas with matching mantles of Celtic wool; and he commissioned statues of him-self to be distributed throughout the city where they could be seen and venerated by everyone. He referred to himself in the third person, an individual he called Jupiter-Amon-Caesar. Still an outspoken atheist he nonetheless showed no compunction at the prospect of bestowing a godship on himself and reminding everyone he was descended directly from Venus. In a way, so what? Any inheritor of royal status understands that somewhere in his lineage is a conqueror. Every king's power is built on subjugation, usually warfare, and not infrequently outright murder. That's how you get there, and that's how you stay.

In 45 BCE Mistress and an entourage that included us cats joined General C in Rome. He put us up at one of his several estates. His wife and children occupied his main lodging and Rome's citizens would have frowned on Mistress living there too. Anyway Mistress had a new husband, Ptolemy XIV, the dead Ptolemy XIII's younger brother and another twerp who was consort and co-regent in name only. The general gave no sign he was worried about incestuous hanky-panky between Mistress and a pre-adolescent boy still yearning for a first pubic hair. Sex is one thing, love another, but then don't take the word of a female cat who loves only when in heat and then shares it freely. Female humans are apparently in heat year-around.

From what I witnessed Mistress and General C were never more than casual sex partners and political allies. Still, satisfying two women in separate parts of town could be tiring for a man in his fifties, especially factoring in Rome's pot-holed streets and the fact that chariot shock absorbers had not yet been invented. The city's more perspicacious observers, notably the acid-tongued gossip, gadfly, and treacherous ass-kisser Cicero, noticed the changes in General C's appearance. He drew attention to the general's countenance, which had become increasingly gray and furrowed, to his diminishing frame and the illogic and confusion apparent in his latest orations. The general had never been a large man, maybe five-feet-three and one hundred-twenty pounds in his prime. Now he appeared shrunken, even vaguely mummified. Perhaps a result of too many hours baking in the desert? Considering the female company he'd kept, Cicero wondered openly if the general could actually prove he had tan lines.

During this time Pompey's two sons reignited the Roman civil war from faraway Spain, but General C dispatched an army and defeated them decisively. He was now in full control of Rome and all its holdings. The Senate pronounced him dictator, and he was preparing to declare himself officially a god until some enemies led by Brutus and Cassius assassinated him with daggers on the Ides of March 44 BCE.

Rome erupted in riots soon after; hooligans and arsonists controlled the streets. Seeing no future for us in Rome, Mistress took us back to Egypt a month later. On arrival she arranged to have her latest husband poisoned and afterward elevated Caesarian, now about three years old and still not potty trained, to co-ruler and calling him Ptolemy XV following the Ptolemaic tradition of naming male successors chronologically. Here he was a co-ruler of all Egypt and still smelled like a dirty diaper. We cats were disgusted. Iras and Charmion could have least pan-trained him.

A précis of the Ptolemaic era would be useful here. It began in 323 BCE with the death of Alexander the Great. This period also brackets the Hellenistic era despite Greece's low profile. The territory Alexander conquered was subsequently partitioned among his generals after his death from malaria, one of whom was Ptolemy I, Alexander's friend since childhood, who was awarded Egypt. Ptolemy I was Macedonian Greek, not Egyptian, and from the start, Greek was the official language of Alexandria rather than Egyptian

Coptic spoken by much of the populace to the south. Obviously the Ptolemies were not direct descendants of Alexander (by this time elevated to a god) as they claimed. Alexander the Great's direct lineage came to a dead end. He left no heirs, his son Alexander IV having been poisoned at age fourteen by rivals, and his many boyfriends proving of no use, the male anus making an imperfect gateway to conception.

The Ptolemaic period lasted roughly three hundred years, ending in 30 BCE with Mistress' suicide as the Roman army of Octavian advanced on her palace. I'll describe that later. She was the last Ptolemaic pharaoh, her son Caesarian and her three children with Antony the first of the line not fathered by a blood relative. During that extended time there had been no outbreeding: family members intermarried as a means of retaining power, although this didn't prevent them from murdering each other during internecine scuffles for prestige, wealth, and hegemony.

The Ptolemaic lineage was no less labyrinthine than the palace intrigues. Mistress had just one set of grandparents because her parents had been brother and sister. These individuals also happened to be uncle and niece. Mistress' grandmother's marriage to her own uncle meant that her father doubled as her brother-in-law. After three centuries a dendrogram of the family tree looked more like a tumbleweed than a stately oak.

This situation, combined with intermittent poisonings and stabbings, should have substantially reduced the number of invitees at family reunions. And in fact it did, to which I can personally attest having attended many of these soirées myself, ordinarily crouched underneath a banquet table awaiting random scraps to fall my way. There can be no question that filial redundancy throughout the Ptolemaic line had a trickle-down effect, resulting in fewer participants at parties than in ordinary families. On the positive side this made more wine and gourmet food available for the survivors. Little wonder most of the men were obese, and not a few of the women. Fortunately for the Ptolemies no overt genetic abnormalities arose as they often do in lineages of pure-bred cats. I never encountered anyone with crossed eyes, hip dysplasia, hemophilia, childhood alopecia, or any such gene-driven malady that might have reduced fitness unless you count malevolence and a peculiar emotional scrofula. However these characters appear as inherent traits of your species worldwide. A cat often toys with a mouse; your bullies play cat-and-mouse with entire continents.

Yes, outbreeding. . . Our voyage home was delayed two days because my brother Anubis had vanished, forcing Mistress, Iras, and Charmion into a frenzied search of the villa and grounds. It was always Anubis the Imp who was a troublemaker, never Aten the Fastidious. Aten was content with life on his pillow, with posing gloriously in sunbeams, yawning and stretching with languorous grace, living in a time-warp that precociously anticipated the portrait photographer. I never wandered unless in heat, and after getting laid I beat it right back to Mistress, who seemed to understand. Anubis? He disappeared into the night at every opportunity wherever we happened to be. No sooner did the sun tumble from the horizon than he was gone, silent as a ghost, and unless we were trapped aboard a ship he was unlikely to return until morning.

The women searched everywhere for him: underneath the furniture, in the shade of bushes, among Mistress' hundreds of pairs of shoes, in General C's bathhouses, and near the birdfeeders where he often hunted. At one point Mistress was actually sobbing, something she never did after sentencing a relative to be tortured, poisoning a prisoner, or ordering a recaptured runaway slave beheaded at her feet. I can't say her tears were shed entirely on Anubis' behalf because we were all stressed by the uncertainty of Rome's political climate.

Mistress was nothing if not pragmatic. Even General C's death left her dry-eyed. After word of his assassination reached her that fateful day she and I closed ourselves in the villa's boudoir while she coolly put pen to papyrus and devised a course of action. For several hours she muttered to herself, scratching her head and pausing over the protean combinations of potential alliances, eventually sketching a decision diagram using "if this, then that" logic. She filled in names of General C's probable successors trying to anticipate how they were likely to perceive her, how amenable they might be to appointing Caesarian as General C's legitimate successor. This last came with legal entanglements because she was not a Roman citizen, nor had she been the general's wife. Caesarian wasn't a citizen of Rome either. Although indisputably Caesar's only known son, he had not been born on Roman soil. When the decision tree reached its apex a single leaf bearing Mark Antony's name stood out. As history records he made a prescient choice, at least over the next few years.

Antony had been visiting our Roman villa occasionally when General C, high on his rhetoric, was addressing the Senate. General C and Antony were on good terms, and his meetings with Mistress were open and platonic. They obviously enjoyed each other's company, flirting obliquely and sipping wine while Antony's chariot and footman waited patiently outside. A friendship based on mutual admiration and trust soon evolved. Also in his favor, Antony was wildly popular in Alexandria for his military prowess and open manner, major advantages in a future consort. Needless to say, Mistress planned ahead. Whether Antony suspected or not, he was already mattress fodder for the Alexandrian boudoir.

As mentioned, Rome was in turmoil immediately following General C's assassination. Another civil war seemed imminent. Political disarray was inevitable despite the bloated encomiums and crocodile tears scattered over Caesar's corpse as it lay in state. The Senate had long been suspicious of what role Mistress might play in General C's new regime, and many of its members openly despised her. To Cicero she was a harlot and interloper not to be trusted. To the masses, having never seen her carried through the streets on a litter, her celebrity, enormous wealth, and exotic status as the goddess Isis (or by religious syncretism, Aphrodite) assigned her to the realm of legend, further fueling the national confusion. Women of the upper classes hated and envied her while simultaneously mimicking her makeup, attire, and hairstyle. These were some of the emotions felt and expressed by various elements of the Roman citizenry, and only General C's powerful presence had allowed her and Caesarian to remain unmolested. Now he was dead. Antony saved Mistress in that critical moment by ensuring our uneventful embarkation.

I for one was ecstatic to leave Rome, a stinking, uncouth, repressed backwater where the narrow streets and twisted alleys stank of offal and dog shit, where people threw garbage and dishwater out their windows. A major social pastime of the upper classes seemed to be disrespecting Alexandrians from afar for their riches, hedonism, and perceived disdain of all things Roman. The embodiment of this widespread sentiment (or call it jealousy) was Mistress. As I alluded earlier the upper classes considered her ambitious, wily, and untrustworthy, a slutty adulteress; in contemporary terminology a rich bitch, and on top of that a foreigner. The underclasses, far removed and unaffected by high-level gossip, moped and coughed in their hutches and scrabbled for scraps in the streets. To them a copper coin represented a fortune.

And the local felid population? On his eventual return Anubis reported Roman street cats to be of low breeding, describing them as flea-ridden and mangy, taken to pawing through piles of curbside trash and seemingly fearful of everything, even the rats that openly scavenged with them. Being a connoisseur of slumming, he was the least eager of us to leave. Finding a female in heat was exciting, well worth the cost of a few scratches and the acquisition of some fleas and ticks. That he eventually became Antony's devoted companion came as no surprise to Aten and me. Many nights they slipped away from the palace together, parting company at one of the side entrances and going their separate ways.

At risk of jumping a few steps in the narrative—to which I promise to return—history knows Mistress chose Antony to replace General C as her own and Egypt's protector. What everyone doesn't know is that she loved him passionately despite his tomcatting tendencies, and he returned that feeling to the extent each elicited in the other a strong cathexis. Once settled in at the palace at Alexandria they often strolled the grounds holding hands and throwing grain to the peafowls, sometimes pausing at fish ponds to stare raptly at their reflections, wondering whatever it is demigods wonder; they whispered in Greek, the language of poetry and music, of piquant senses and sly titillation. Left unspoken was a mutual understanding that power is the ultimate aphrodisiac.

3

What was he like? Momentarily disregard the notion of his godlike eminence and consider Antony the mortal. I would describe him as tall by standards of the time, about five-feet-six and one hundred-forty pounds. Statues are invariably outsized, offering little useful information about actual dimensions of their subjects. Those carved while Antony was alive depict a man with the standard Roman nose, blank eyeballs, and stocky build. In contrast with General C, Antony sported a full head of hair, but of course he was also much younger. His hair was arranged in a ferocious coiffure of curls, appealing, I suppose, if you admire a head topped with ten pounds of earthworms engaged in frantic group sex. Another example where a sculptor tried hard to chisel motion into his statuary and failed. But then cats hardly qualify as art critics. What I'm offering is personal opinion. I saw a few of these likenesses myself here in Alexandria and must say that I've never gotten the point of representation.

Cats don't much notice a human's looks. What matters to us is olfaction. With exception of perfumed specimens such as Mistress every human smells distinctive to a cat. I'll tell you this: Antony had intriguing body odor, strong enough to knock a charging rhinoceros to its knees. In Rome, had I been a wanderer, I could have located him by his scent even at the Colosseum among the inebriated, slobbering hordes in their stinking togas and reeking sandals. Not even the crowded gladiator quarters smelled as rank as Antony standing alone in the open air. General C's odor had been less noticeable, more an old man smell. I figured that if Mistress liked her men gamey it was none of my business.

Caesar's insatiable curiosity had been nearly palpable. He was fascinated by how the Nile's level rose then fell just before the growing season, leaving behind a fresh layer of nutrient-laden soil on the floodplains. Egypt starved during years when the river failed to breach its banks. Then there was coastal Alexandria, the most cosmopolitan city in the world, throbbing with the energy of immigrants bringing a continuous infusion of wealth and diversity. It was a smorgasbord of languages, cultures, entertainments, religions, knowledge, and currencies, and the general wanted to absorb it all. When the palace had been besieged he studied the latest war machines through a window in Mistress' boudoir, conscripting several of her male Latin-speaking slaves to infiltrate the mob below and discover what sorts of ropes propelled the latest model of catapults. Were the torsion springs the traditional skeins of sinew with their superior range of tension or some other material discovered since his absence from Rome? What was the design of the trigger mechanism? How many turns of the windlass were needed to cock the apparatus, and how many did it take to turn it? The devices were clearly effective, hurling ten-pound stones from a hundred yards that regularly dinged the palace walls. I remember Mistress and Charmion laughing as he stood naked before the window, his back to us, the effulgence of his bare ass heightened by a sunbeam. He was fully immersed in the moment and oblivious to everything but the scene before him, toga crumpled and forgotten on the floor.

In his time General C had been the greatest soldier and military strategist alive, a brave warrior loved and admired by his men; Antony was thought to be right behind him and the general's probable successor, although some members of the Senate had criticized his skill as a strategist. Both men were ardent admirers of women, and both were profligate and usually in debt. Aside from these character traits they had little in common. General C was stern, cerebral, curious, superbly educated, and highly organized, an apperceptive scholar in a warrior's clothing. Antony was earthy and self-deprecating, a sensualist. He was a lover of opulence, laughter, and pranks, tending to drink too much and make a fool of himself, benign and even endearing qualities to Alexandrians but seen as vulgar in Rome's more dour culture. He was a

Hellenistic frat boy, once hitching his chariot to a pair of tame lions and joyriding drunkenly through the streets of Rome to the delight and amazement of the citizens. One time while seated in the Senate following an all-night debauch he opened his mouth to speak but puked into his lap instead. The sententious Cicero lambasted him for weeks afterward.

Shortly after his murder General C's will was read aloud in Pompey's former villa where Antony was currently squatting. Antony had already given away its tapestries and furniture and he and his cronies were using the place as a party house. Terms of the will provided for the general's family, but left the estate where we Alexandrians had been living temporarily to the Roman people along with seventy-five drachmas to every adult male citizen. Foreigners by law could not be heirs, and the will did not mention Caesarian or Mistress. Also omitted for unstated reasons was Antony, whose extravagant lifestyle and frequent drunkenness had evidently made him, in General C's opinion, untrustworthy to lead. Instead the general appointed his grandnephew Octavian, a callow teenager of eighteen, as his official heir by legally adopting him and giving him the name Caesar. He tapped Antony to be Octavian's guardian. Antony was pissed, having envisioned himself as General C's legally adopted son. Caesar, in choosing Octavian, bequeathed not just his name but inserted him directly into his family's lineal descent from Venus. This happened in a time when biological kinships with immortals could be decreed; that is, well before Mendelian genetics came along and ruined things for rulers pining to be Earthly gods and goddesses. Beginning at that moment Octavian and Antony felt nothing but mutual execration.

I said that Antony was pissed at being passed over, but more accurately he was enraged. In his panegyric at General C's funeral he excoriated the general's assassins, igniting riots, arson, looting, and random deaths in the streets. Citizens retreated behind locked doors and shuttered windows. There were calls for the Senate to track down the murderers and bring them to justice. Cicero, never an admirer of the general, defamed him obliquely by damning Mistress for Rome's newest troubles. He was especially concerned because Mistress was visibly pregnant, having amply reinforced her filial ties to the fertility goddess Isis. Because the conception had occurred on Roman soil an argument could be made for a male child being General C's legal heir, a possibility that drove Cicero nearly to apoplexy.

The threat became moot when Mistress later miscarried. Exactly when and where this event occurred—at sea or back in Alexandria—history doesn't record, nor is sex of the fetus mentioned, but I know. A week out of port our vessel became trapped in a violent spring storm. I was curled up in the berth with Mistress when she went into preterm labor and expelled the dead fetus and its placenta. For obvious political reasons the fetus, which was female, was dropped overboard in the night, and Iras and Charmion were sworn to secrecy. The world never knew.

In November 43 BCE Octavian and Antony came to a nervous truce and merged their militaries. They also included Lepidus, who brought with him an experienced army. The framework for this new triumvirate was hammered out during two days and two nights of intense negotiation during which the three generals declared themselves emperors and carved the Roman world into thirds. This alliance became necessary because Brutus and Cassius, leaders of the group that assassinated General C, had reached an accord of their own. Antony was still vengeful about the murder of his friend and mentor despite the disappointment of having been screwed out of an inheritance. Octavian wanted revenge because as General C's adopted son letting Brutus and Cassius to go unpunished was an insult to his step-father's memory. Lepidus was interested only in the money.

How did all this affect Mistress? Having once been General C's consort she was a ready-made enemy of Brutus and Cassius, who would eventually attack Egypt and try to topple her throne. Octavian and Lepidus were unknown quantities, but Antony had once been her friend and protector and might be again in this new alliance. As cats we couldn't have cared less about these ridiculous intrigues. When you're a cat, even a pampered cat, the streets always beckon. Cats are survivors. Wars cause urban rodent populations to explode, so even if cats themselves don't organize for the purpose of killing each other, we love it when one human civilization destroys another. That means more rats and mice for everybody.

The triumvirate now needed money to achieve its main two goals of expansion and avenging General C. They independently drew up hit lists of prominent Romans who were either wealthy or personal enemies. There was some trading back and forth, as in I'll kill that asshole neighbor of yours if you agree to have my mother-in-law thrown alive into the sewers. Antony managed to get Cicero on the list in exchange for one of his own uncles, but what the hell, some collateral damage is inevitable.

The carnage began as soon as the triumvirate returned to Rome. Blood, as the trite phrase goes, ran freely in the streets. Again the citizens cowered, afraid even to come out of hiding long enough to bury the dead. Corpses were tossed into the Tiber or left rotting to be picked apart by birds and stray dogs. The hit list lengthened as names of acquaintances that were simply irritating or unpleasant were added, or that were irritating or unpleasant to friends and relatives or the friends and relatives of friends and relatives. Cicero got his comeuppance. Antony saw to his beheading and that his head and the hands he'd used to clutch his poisonous pens were displayed prominently in the Senate. By the time the final drops of blood trickled into the gutters, several thousand citizens had been executed, including a third of the sitting senators. The triumvirs now stood alone and unopposed, backed by forty-three legions. They were also broke. Booty scavenged from the dead and appropriated from those still living wasn't enough to pay the bills. The big money was elsewhere: in a word, Egypt.

Less than a year later the triumvirate defeated Brutus and Cassius in eastern Macedonia in the two battles of Philippi. Victory was decisive. From the standpoint of political theory autocracy carried the day. Republicanism—and with it democracy and any glimmer of personal freedom—had lost. After their defeat, Brutus and Cassius committed suicide to prevent capture, as was customary. Antony fought bravely. Octavian showed up after the second conflict ended in time to order Brutus' head removed for display in Rome, but the trophy was lost in transit. Damned unfortunate.

Antony and Octavian parted ways with Lepidus and signed a contract dividing the immediate world between them. Antony, the burly and undisputed hero of Philippi, was now a demigod. He was forty-two and in his prime, a soldier's soldier. Octavian in comparison was physically weak and sallow, cowardly even, not a wisp of a warrior. He was sickly, burdened by a history of undefined illnesses, and physically unimposing. He was skinny and even with sandal-lifts was shorter than General C. But perhaps his greatest deficiency was a hard and withered heart.

Octavian was depressing and unpleasant to be around: charmless, duplicitous, dead-eyed, dainty in personal habits to the point of femininity. Unlike

Antony he was abstemious and antisocial at gatherings, observing the other guests as a hungry snake assesses a roomful of rats to identify the most vulnerable. He was paranoid about being assassinated, no doubt with good reason, and trusted few people. Honor was anathema; he was a cunning and ruthless prevaricator. Despite Antony's greater popularity, respect, and openly honest manner, Octavian's far less admirable traits proved superior in the end.

I've told you something of Antony's and Octavian's characters and sketched the outline of Mistress', but how did she come across to others? As a complex person, certainly, by her late teens a master negotiator and administrator capable of controlling currencies and arranging political alliances beneficial to Egypt and to herself. She sought every advantage, overt or subtle. Although not a great beauty, her perfumes were legendary, her grace, charm, and intelligence unmatched. In sum, she was a tantalizing presence. Since childhood she had been schooled by tutors in oratory and drama, and she knew Greek history and poetry as well as anyone. Her direct gaze suggested forthrightness while dissembling what it was she felt; her calm demeanor disarmed interlocutors making them feel safe as if they had been lifelong friends. When she spoke—and she was a polyglot fluent in at least nine languages, including several barbarian tongues—the world heard a soft, melodic voice. In conversation she was never without a riposte or *bot mon*, which no doubt irritated and perhaps even intimidated the great Cicero, whose own greatest skills might have been abasement and calumny. Her wardrobe was fulsome as befitting a queen, her carriage that of a goddess, perhaps not surprising considering she had been born one.

She not so much walked as floated, white slippers seeming barely to touch the ground. When appearing in public she dressed as the Earthly incarnation of Isis. Raucous crowds gathered to gape as her litter moved slowly down Alexandria's Canopic Way. When she rose and stood motionless and unsmiling, turning occasionally to face the opposite side, right arm raised in the Egyptian salute, the citizens were dazzled into near silence, their shouts replaced by an undercurrent of soft murmurs overlain with the labored breathing and shuffling feet of the slaves bearing her litter and the creaking of its carrying poles; the only remnants of her passing were faint whispers of Indian silk and an inchoate memory of perfume, the source of which remained forever a mystery. Cleopatra's palace banquets were served on heavy settings of gold and silver, which she afterward gave to her guests as gifts. At one banquet the dinnerware was said to weigh three hundred tons. If the guests were foreign military officers she might also present each with a war horse draped in silver trappings along with two male slaves, one to lead the horse by its gem-studded halter, the other to hold a torch to light the way.

Antony's victory at Philippi drenched Macedonia's eastern plain with the blood of thousands. People love a winner and in Rome winning wars was how you stayed atop the popularity polls. Out of boredom he decided to invade and conquer the Persian Empire, at that time called Parthia, but he needed money plus an additional army, his own having been sorely diminished. Egypt might supply both. The only unknown factor was whether he could sweet-talk Mistress into bankrolling his venture, or so he thought.

Antony was handsome, his personality magnetic, and women had always been drawn to him. He counted on cashing in the personal capital banked from schmoozing with Mistress in Rome. Thus relying entirely on his macho reputation and proven charm he summoned her to meet him at Tarsus in modern southern Turkey where he had gone to loaf after Philippi and rest for a time on his accolades. The trouble with loafing is that it sometimes leads to planning, and not infrequently plans born of ennui are stupid. There was no logical reason to approach this particular nest of wasps called Parthia and give it a whack; richer, easier targets were available nearby.

Mistress recognized she had no dog in this fight Antony proposed. Still, Egypt needed his protection. Antony was arguably the most powerful individual in the Mediterranean world, his only possible rival being Octavian. Angering him was obviously not wise, but from her standpoint neither was girlish capitulation an option. There were other ways of assuaging his wishes besides underwriting an ill-advised war in which she had much to lose and nothing to gain. A good deal of Egypt's wealth was invested in its military, and the prospect of losing part of it unnecessarily was not appealing.

Mistress was a hostess nonpareil, and no one played the international game of thrust and feint with more dexterity. There have been women famous for doing a lot with a little, but to do even more with everything? History has no match. She decided to accept Antony's summons, which to his credit had been worded delicately as a formal invitation and not a command. He mentioned Parthia and other possibilities offering endless riches and hinted at a partnership, the details to be decided when they met.

Mistress was naturally interested, but acceptance of the invitation would be on her terms. We were in the boudoir when the message arrived by courier. Mistress read it and set it aside on her desk. It had come on a day of no meetings, so she was lounging around without makeup. She ran her fingers through her hair, which badly needed a wash, and started to pen a response before pausing and setting the pen down. "No," she muttered to us, her felid confidants. "I'll let him sweat a little."

She told Charmion to dismiss the courier, sending him back to Tarsus without a reply. She picked up the pen and started doodling, making little hieroglyphs while talking to herself. "I'll figure the trip at roughly five hundred nautical miles, including some necessary tacking. Skirting Cyprus also adds some distance," she said.

Allow me, Annipe, a word of explanation here. In the ancient world even approximate measures of distance and time were unknown, time being measured in days, whatever those were. Obviously the nautical mile, hour, minute, and so forth did not yet exist, but for simplicity I'll assume for a minute (pardon me) they did. To measure fractions of a day there was the water clock, called a *clepsydra* in Greek. The potential of "telling time" offered intriguing opportunities. A famous courtesan in Athens was known as "The Clepsydra" because she used one of these devices to schedule her clients. I shall say no more. Details of her story are best discussed under the rubric of technology and irrelevant here.

Mistress looked across the room at nothing in particular. She crossed one leg over the other and started the foot bouncing up and down, displacement activity she often employed while concentrating. "Unless the vessel sinks or he pulls in at Cyprus to visit some bimbo. . ." Her voice trailed off as she made a few calculations on the papyrus. Mistress, keep in mind, was familiar with navigation and sailing having been educated in mathematics and geometry. As to the practical side she personally commanded the Egyptian navy.

"If the courier returns to Tarsus by the shortest distance instead of hugging the coast his course tracks north-northeast," she muttered. "Let's assume a reliable northwesterly wind striking the port side of the ship obliquely, not unreasonable during the warm months. I'm presuming that even the crappiest square sail arrangement can be close-hauled into the wind within one point (11°15') keeping the ship on a reach. After factoring in a little eastward slippage. . ." For a minute or two she scribbled quickly, her foot moving faster. "At a sustained 2 knots he should be kneeling at Antony's feet inside ten days." The foot came to a stop. She thoughtfully chewed the feathered end of her pen and gazed out the window. After a moment she stood, called to Charmion, and went to take a bath.

"I believe there's a sea voyage in our future," I whispered telepathically, but as usual my brothers had slept through everything.

4

The courier came twice more only to be sent away without a response. Mistress left the invitations stacked on her desk. The third time I could hear him in the hall begging Charmion to please convince Mistress to respond or he was likely to lose his head. He meant this literally. Antony, he said, had taken to pacing back and forth in his chambers, drinking and cursing his staff and abusing his slaves. These were not propitious signs.

The time was right to strike. Mistress sat down and immediately penned a response. She wrote that she'd be delighted to meet Antony in Tarsus and discuss mutual business interests over a roasted stuffed hog and maybe a glass or two, and she'd start preparing to leave Alexandria at once. Several weeks were required to organize everything for the trip, implying that a girl needs time to pack. Plus she had business demands here at home: there were taxes to collect, grain inventories to check and confirm, some of the natives to the south were restless and needed to be lined up and flogged. . . She begged his patience and signed off.

She next summoned the admiral of her navy and ordered him to dispatch carpenters, riggers, sailmakers, shipwrights, camp cooks, procurers, a construction supervisor, and a contingent of marines to guard them to the mouth of the Cydnus River ten miles downstream of Tarsus. There the supervisor was to buy a commercial barge in good condition and outfit it to resemble a slightly smaller version of her royal barges. She would use it to make her entrance into the city, where Antony would be waiting. Her royal vessels were suited only for calm inland waters and not seaworthy. When the rebuilt barge was finished the supervisor was to send word, at which time she would arrive with her fleet of seagoing quadriremes loaded with accoutrements to decorate and stage it. Mistress, I need not remind you, was also trained in stage-setting. She anticipated the splendor of her arrival in Tarsus exceeding even General C's Roman triumphs, parades unmatched for color and ostentation.

Once embarked, our entourage took its time following the coast east and north. The compass, invented centuries earlier in China, was still unknown in the West. Although direct crossings of the Mediterranean were not uncommon, mariners of our time preferred sailing with coastal landmarks in sight, putting into port at night to keep from running aground. There were few lighthouses, and nighttime navigation in our cumbersome ships was risky. This also gave

Mistress time to meet with her various business and political interests enroute. Before leaving she had given orders that we cats were not permitted shore leave, probably a good idea because I was in heat and confined to one of her shipboard closets. She couldn't risk waiting around in case one of us—namely Anubis or I—returned late.

Our fleet dropped anchor near the refitted barge, and Mistress' staging crew went immediately to work transforming it into a floating palace. The Cydnus River ran clear and cold out of the Taurus Mountains, a far more attractive setting than the sluggish, muddy Nile.

On a bright morning we set off upriver powered by an elite team of oarsmen, sunlight glinting off the vessel's gilded stern and silver-tipped oars. So we cats could enjoy the open air our tray of sand had been set atop the eponymous poop deck. The oarsmen rowed slowly, steadily, and in perfect synchrony, blades dipping and rising silently like the necks of feeding swans. Mistress, clothed as Venus, reclined underneath a purple canopy on a flaming red couch affecting a fetching pose with head tipped back and black hair tumbling to the sides while beautiful young slave boys dressed as cupids fanned her. We sat beside Mistress in our Egyptian-cat poses while Iras and Charmion stood nearby in translucent white tunics, one to each side. Scattered about the deck were lithe slave girls in the attire of nymphs, singing sweetly and playing harps and lyres. The sail, dyed royal purple, had been heavily perfumed. It was allowed to luff while its ropes hung limply, the better to distribute its aroma to the masses lining both riverbanks. As the barge approached Tarsus everyone abandoned the central marketplace and ran to the harbor to view this once-in-a-lifetime spectacle. Antony was left sitting alone on his dais.

Our approach had been masterful; apparently even Antony was rendered speechless when he finally jettisoned his pride and went to see for himself. As the ungainly barge approached the dock the crowd noise attenuated, leaving only sweet music drifting toward the city. Suddenly a boatswain barked a command. Instantly the oarsmen below the first deck lifted their oars, held them horizontally for a count of two, and retracted them in perfect unison through the oarports. Shipping of the oars was silent because the tholepins had been padded with leather, eliminating the usual clattering of wood on wood. The maneuver was repeated quickly in sequence by the second deck crew, then the third, until all oars on the starboard side had disappeared inside the ship. The craft slid gently to the dock and stopped within inches of touching it. Everything had been accomplished with exquisite precision. The crowd gasped, then roared. Mistress rose slowly off her couch, stood imperiously like the goddess she was, and gave the Egyptian salute.

Once the barge had docked Antony sent a courier asking Mistress to dine with him in town that night, but she parried with an invitation of her own to join him on the barge instead. Astounded and amused at this audacity, he accepted.

The bash matched and probably even exceeded Mistress' reputation as western civilization's premier hostess. She had decorated the barge's several banquet rooms with dozens of couches draped in expensive silks of different colors. The wealthy classes of that day sat or lay on couches to dine, picking morsels from dishes and bowls and drinking from goblets set before them. There was no cutlery; everything served was finger-food. In this case the dinnerware was Mistress' usual heavy gold and silver decorated with inlaid semi-precious stones. Antony, although no country boy, was clearly flabbergasted by the spread, and he and his generals fell to. Everything Antony saw, she told him, he could take with him afterward. The entire display was a gift.

The banquet itself was as ravishing as its hostess. Set before her guests were roasted pigs, skins baked and crinkled to perfection, their abdomens stuffed with ducks, thrushes, mussels, and oysters; buckets of salted hummingbird tongues accompanied by honey sauce mixed with cinnamon for dipping; skeins of freshly made sausages draped over the arms of voluptuous slave girls circling among the couches; grilled fishes caught that day and dusted with paprika, black pepper, and other rare spices; salted herrings and smoked mackerels from the cold seas of Spain; breads hot from shipboard ovens; kids seethed in the milk of their mothers and stuffed with sweetbreads flavored with basil and rosemary. Around the edges of the rooms stood giant amphorae filled with the Mediterranean's finest wines hovered over by wine stewards who never let anyone's cup remain empty. There were also sweet wines made from Judean dates, the finest in the Mediterranean world.

To cool both drink and brow in that intense midsummer heat was perhaps the most remarkable treat of all. Mistress had sent agents ahead who arranged for a pack train of donkeys to travel back and forth from the Taurus Mountains carrying saddlebags laden with snow. There was enough that Mistress sent her slaves into the crowded streets with papyrus cones filled with honey-flavored snow for distribution to the people. After that night the city was hers: she was indeed a goddess, and a generous one.

The scene was repeated with variations in the menu during the next four nights, except that on the fourth night Antony and his entourage stepped into the banquet rooms to find themselves knee-deep in freshly cut roses. In the stifling summer heat of Tarsus the sweet scent was whelming and simultaneously unforgettable. At the end of every night Antony returned to shore laden as usual with priceless dinnerware and furnishings. Mistress even gave him the couches and their coverings along with the tables and tapestries. Stored in the hold of her quadrireme was a nearly endless supply of everything needed to throw a party, and nobody ever had to wash the dishes.

That night Antony stayed over. She watched him

openly fondling her slave girls after the other guests left and knew monogamy was futile, but that wasn't the game anyway. The game—the great game—was acquisition of power, and she knew as well as anyone how to play it. Antony's godlike status after Philippi, plus his military authority and prowess, would be enough to rally whatever support they needed to double-team the world into subjugation. It was critical that her own country buy into this impending partnership.

Egyptian tradition called for a queen to be accompanied by a male consort and co-regent, preferably someone recognized and respected by everyone. These need not be the same individual, as I shall explain later. And it helped if this personage (or personages) had already achieved divine status or were at least on the threshold of godhood. Antony's résumé checked all these boxes. If only she could keep him focused and sober enough to follow her lead. Eventually they toddled off to the boudoir, Mistress clear-headed, Antony shitfaced and tripping in his sandals over imaginary obstacles.

We cats stayed behind in the banquet rooms pawing through the crushed roses in search of scraps. The guests had gotten pretty loaded, and what fell from their plates and mouths was enough for another banquet. We found ourselves in competition with some oarsmen who had sneaked up from below decks, also attracted by the leftovers. As I view the scene in retrospect we must have presented a strange sight: three cats and a hundred or so half-naked slaves on their hands and knees jabbering in a dozen languages, all of us scavenging shoulder to shoulder on a rose-covered floor.

Eventually the oarsmen returned to the heat and stink of their cramped quarters beneath us. We crept into the boudoir but stayed away from the bed, still wary of Antony's repressed violence. The room was silent. We figured they were finally asleep, Mistress nursing a sore pussy, but that would have discounted the multiple facets of human sexuality. We cats do it cat-style, and that's about it. Suddenly Antony bellowed like a bull being castrated. "*Wow!*" we heard him exclaim. "That's the best blowjob I've had *in my life*! Not even my Babylonian slave girl can match it. You know, the one with green eyes?"

"I hadn't noticed the color of her eyes," Mistress said with an undertone of asperity.

"Now I understand why Uncle C—I can hardly call him 'Dad' because of that scurrilous little prick Octavian—held you in such high esteem."

Mistress said, "And here I attributed his attachment entirely to my charm and intellect, the fact that I'm a helluva savvy ruler, and the dazzling Greek vocabulary I used when perfervidly expressing admiration of his own considerable achievements."

"Well, of course, and because you give a *really* good blowjob."

Mistress didn't reply, but I knew she was thinking about her next move, lying there in the darkness.

Antony sat up, sounding sober now. "I've made

a decision," he said. "I'm going back to Alexandria with you. This is just too damn good to leave behind. Fuck the Parthians, I can always start a war with those wogs."

Mistress hugged him and told him what a man he was, not just handsome and strong with a tight butt, but a terrific lover as well. She said she couldn't be happier. There was one little thing he might do for her: get rid of her little sister Arsinoë, the remaining sibling still alive and last potential threat to her throne. Arsinoë had sought sanctuary in the Temple of Artemis at Ephesus a thousand kilometers directly west of Tarsus. We heard Mistress yelp and Antony yawn and roll onto his side. He'd evidently given her a titty-twister. Within a minute he was snoring.

The next morning he sent word to have Arsinoë dragged out of the temple—sacrilege by anyone's definition—and executed on its marble steps. He also ordered her few supporters to be dispatched along with a charlatan claiming to be Ptolemy XIII, Mistress' younger brother and first husband whose body was never found after the battle of his forces against General C's. Mistress, who valued family ties about as much as us cats, was ecstatic. The remaining competition—whether genuine or not—was now eliminated.

Back at the palace Antony fell into extended bouts of drunkenness and acedia, subject to eidetic dreams in which an unknown goddess descended to his bedside and held his hand, whispering that he too could become immortal. Ever the professional soldier, war seemed the only activity capable of leveling his attention. Alexandria was an exciting city, but at the time it had no wars. Mistress was a shrewd interpreter of the human psyche. She knew Antony to be an honest, simple man who needed a nudge now and then. He craved nearly constant entertainment and hated being alone. Luckily she was a chameleon. General C had wanted an intellectual equal, a charmer and negotiator of his own caliber, a queen of divine heritage and regal manner, and he had gotten all this. Antony wanted a pal, a classy woman but still able to laugh at his barracks humor and even match it; a gamine someone willing to set aside her royal stature when low entertainment presented. To his delight he'd found her: Mistress shifted easily from silk and perfume to coarse fabric and the stench of the masses.

They amused themselves by going on beach picnics, playing dice, fishing from the royal barges, hunting, practicing military exercises, horseback riding, eating and drinking, attending chariot and horse races, and venturing forth on nocturnal sprees through the slums. Dressed as servants they knocked on random doors playing tricks on the occupants. Many times they came home bearing scratches and bruises acquired while scuffling with members of the lower classes, illiterates who took them for the fools and louts they pretended to be.

Following these drunken episodes they returned to the palace laughing and leaning on each other. On entering the Queen's chambers with a snootful,

Antony enjoyed wrestling good-naturedly with his Roman soldiers standing guard, often rolling around with them on the floor, punching them and allowing them to punch him. This was another example of how he treated his men like confrères instead of the uneducated foot soldiers they were, and this more than wages bought their loyalty. They adored him.

Afterward he flopped onto the bed fully clothed and stinking and commenced to snore. Meanwhile Iras and Charmion nervously drew Mistress a perfumed bath and disposed of her clothing. If Anubis happened to have stayed in that evening or come home early he curled up on Antony's chest. Not even the potent scent of Mistress' bath water could mask a body odor like Antony's. While Anubis drifted off in blissful anosmia Aten and I moved to the adjacent bedroom knowing Mistress would soon be joining us.

A couple of times we took leisurely trips south lasting two weeks or so, living aboard one of the royal barges. These episodes were meant to reinforce Mistress' divine status to the Egyptian people and that of her co-regent Antony, who now considered himself the incarnation of Dionysus/Osiris, the Greek god of wine and fertility and Earthly consort of Isis/Aphrodite. Along the way mistress met with magistrates and the managers of her many business enterprises to discuss harvests and taxes; she also worshipped at different temples, leaving gifts and obtaining the blessings of the priests.

Trailing behind the royal barge were some four

hundred other vessels bearing functionaries and their functionaries, guests with their own entourages, and whatever else was necessary for a two-week luxury trip up the Nile. Fresh foods could be bought along the way, but our flotilla carried sufficient supplies to feed everyone, including the thousands of slaves and hired servants who were oarsmen, slave masters, carpenters, blacksmiths, shipwrights, secretaries, threshers, librarians, sailmakers, riggers, rope and basket makers, deck hands, navigators, naval officers, clerks, priests, fishermen, whores, boatswains, pre-pubescent boys to service the male Greek and Arab guests, physicians, charioteers, mechanics, surgeons, tanners, shoemakers, bakers, pharmacists, chandlers, wet nurses, net menders, stable hands, hand maidens, hairdressers, chambermaids, barbers, saddlers and tack makers, shepherds, cooks, food servers, butlers, laundry workers, bath and bathroom attendants, seamstresses, maître d's, sommeliers, rhetoricians and orators, poultry keepers, pest exterminators, butchers, grocers, pursers, purchasing agents, eunuchs, accountants, tailors, tutors, scholars, musicians, actors, stage-setters, stagehands, ink and dye makers, tasters, translators, poets, singers, magicians, soothsayers, mimes, jugglers, jesters, tumblers, dancers, guard dogs and their handlers, sword sharpeners, gladiators, fools. . . The list was endless. We were a city and entertainment complex on the move.

I almost forgot that Antony brought along one of his legions stationed in Alexandria so he had Roman soldiers to command and Latin-speaking drinking companions during periods of boredom. Wherever we docked he amused himself by putting his men ashore and running them through a series of military exercises. This impressed and delighted the locals, few of whom had ever seen a Roman soldier, much less an army of them. Our Nubian came too, of course, carrying us in our basket. As always, one necessary accoutrement was a silver tray and enough white Mediterranean beach sand to last the duration. Mistress had no intention of making us shit in damp floodplain loam.

The royal barge we usually took on these excursions measured three hundred feet, the length of a modern American football field, although not quite the width. Voyaging south on the Nile meant pushing against the current flowing north to the Mediterranean, which impeded progress. The effort was somewhat offset by a steady northerly blowing upriver, allowing the square mainsails to be set perpendicular to the wind. In addition to sails the vessel was a quadrireme propelled by three tiers of oarsmen, some positioned two to an oar, who lifted, lowered, and pulled their oars in unison. How many were aboard? I never counted, but certainly hundreds. The craft hardly qualified as ocean-going. It was, as history describes, strictly for pleasure on calm waters, and if taken to sea would likely have capsized even in a middling storm. Mistress berthed it and its sister duplicates among a thousand or more attendant boats at Lake Mareotis just south of Alexandria. The port was connected by canals to the Nile and Egypt's southern interior.

These vessels were in actuality floating palaces no less glorious than the structure they exemplified. They might have been the most opulent floating party crafts ever built. Amenities? A typical ship rose two levels, the decks connected by spiral staircases. Throughout were gilded, intricately carved statues. Everywhere were panels of polished wood and pink granite; the handrails, balustrades, and furniture were inlaid with ivory and gold. Imposing colonnades of white marble nearly twenty feet tall lined the railings from bow to stern. Hundreds of elephants had donated their ivory to inlay the ship's prows; the fittings were polished bronze, the enormous sails sewn from triple-backed linen dyed royal purple.

Each barge contained numerous bedrooms, a gymnasium, a library with attending librarians, stables, banquet rooms, baths and bathrooms staffed with attendants, and much more. It was, I said, a city. The Nile's water being muddy and unappealing, a swimming pool on the first deck held clear water fit to drink from Alexandrian wells, plus an additional volume stored in a tank on the second deck. Water from the tank could be drained by gravity through a clever system of valves into the pool, maintaining its level as needed. Every kitchen (there were several) was staffed around the clock by cooks, servers, sommeliers, scullery slaves, a chief steward, and a maître d. There were wine storage closets, shrines to Dionysus and Aphrodite, steam baths, gardens, a grotto, a chariot garage and repair shop, and, as mentioned earlier, stables to house horses and sacrificial animals. Extispicy was still practiced, and sheep in particular were favorites of the shipboard soothsayers who slayed them and observed the internal organs, interpreting how they lay as windows into the future. Our barge even had an aquarium housing giant Nile perches each weighing perhaps a hundred pounds. To keep them from suffocating alternating teams of slaves pumping foot bellows injected air into the water throughout the day and night.

No wonder Antony tarried instead of returning to Rome and the cesspool of its politics. Then news came that the Parthians had invaded Syria, making them a potential threat to Egypt. It was April 40 BCE and he had just turned forty-three. At the same time Fulvia, Antony's wife, had teamed with his brother and started a war with Octavian in Italy. She had two motives: prodding Antony to leave Mistress and return home, and stimulating his flagging ambition. Both required defeating Octavian. However both generals were still bound by a mutual nonaggression contract, which Fulvia had just violated. She believed her husband ought to rule the whole Mediterranean world, not just the eastern half.

Octavian quickly subdued Fulvia's troops and she fled to Greece. On the march in Syria Antony received a message from his wife detailing her defeat. This was the first he had heard about her ruse against

Octavian. He immediately abandoned his Parthian mission and went to her aid in Greece, where she was afraid Octavian would murder her and their children. On arriving Antony upbraided her then left without a farewell for the Adriatic with his newly minted Egyptian fleet paid for and built by Mistress, leaving Fulvia in Sicyon where she died a few months later of an unknown illness.

Mistress had expected Antony's return to Alexandria, but what is now history intervened. Pompey's son Sextus and his fleet had blocked grain shipments to Rome, and festering civil unrest had destroyed Italy's agriculture. Romans were starving, causing Octavian's popularity to plunge. He still had the upper hand with Antony because his wife had broken their peace treaty. In October that same year they held a parley in Misenum near Naples and devised a new one. Now that Antony was a widower and to seal the pact Octavian offered his half-sister Octavia in marriage. Antony accepted. Octavia was twenty-nine and a widow. In addition to her beauty Octavia was graceful, calm, and perhaps most important, apolitical, unlikely to ever pull a stunt like Fulvia's and drop everyone's ass into boiling oil. Octavian and Antony were now brothers-in-law, although still openly despising each other. Neither wanted a war, at least not at the moment.

The marriage took place in Rome at the end of December. Naturally word reached Alexandria. Was Mistress pissed when she read the message? That nobody in the palace actually died or suffered a mortal wound was miraculous. I never saw her so angry and distraught. She fumed and stormed around the boudoir screaming curses and throwing perfume bottles at Iras and Charmion, who took refuge in the bathtub. My brothers and I darted past the guards into the hall and ran to daylight. Once outdoors we hid under some bushes, not creeping back to the Queen's chambers until well after dark. By then the three women were drunk, crying pitifully, and holding each other. We had never before seen Mistress with her makeup in such disarray. Her face in the dim light appeared to be melting underneath the tears.

Anubis took one quick glance at the scene and departed for the streets, never to return. He walked directly past the guards standing by the door and down the corridor. That was the last we saw of him. Aten and I jumped onto the bed hoping to provide comfort, although both of us felt our lives might be compromised at any moment. Eventually Mistress flopped onto the bedspread and fell asleep with the two of us curled against her.

Her behavior to us seemed strange. Mistress had always been catlike in dealing with other humans, by this I mean indifferent and unemotional, even distant. This applied as well to her offspring, who stayed in their own quarters in another section of the palace under the care of nurses and tutors who satisfied all their needs, who even when they were small and teething gave them fried mice to chew on. She rarely saw or asked about them. I know for a fact that she had only two lovers in her lifetime despite what the gossips in Rome were saying and writing. Sex with General C was just part of their business arrangement, another day at the office. I wouldn't have been surprised to see them shaking hands after fucking. Antony? Now that was another matter. Antony was a stud. She started caterwauling almost before he stuck it to her and didn't stop until he finally rolled off.

Those times were actually when I felt closest to her, although being humped by only one tom in a single night was beyond my understanding or experience. Whenever I was in heat they lined up and waited their turns. Whoring wasn't in Mistress' nature as it was in mine. She was a creature of thoughts, I purely a victim of hormones. She popped five children into the world counting General C's stillborn fetus; I'd produced five litters before age three.

Before dawn Mistress went into labor and later that morning gave birth to fraternal twins, a boy and girl, fathered by Antony. Childbirth—twins no less—and a hellacious hangover in the same morning would kill most women but Mistress was beyond tough. She named the boy Alexander Helios to honor the sun, the girl Cleopatra Selene after the moon. News of the birth of Alexander Helios caused a sensation in the male-dominated western world. His circumstances were irresistible. Here was a true thoroughbred, a son of Mark Antony who ruled half the world (including Egypt), an admired general and god, descended he claimed at the time, from Hercules. Alexander Helios was also a lineal descent of another god, Alexander the Great (which actually he wasn't; Alexander left no heirs), and his half-brother Caesarian was the mighty Caesar's only son. His exotic mother, the most powerful woman on Earth and wealthy beyond imagination, sat on Egypt's throne, the living incarnation of Isis.

5

We didn't see Antony for nearly four years. Octavian and he had settled their differences for the moment, but each warily eyed the other, and neither went anywhere without a dagger hidden in his tunic. Octavia gave birth to Antony's daughter in 39 BCE, which relieved Mistress who rightly feared competition for her sons from a male child.

Across the Mediterranean the Parthians were sizing up Egypt—at one time part of the earlier Persian Empire—and licking their lips now that Antony wasn't lurking in the background. Except that he was. Mistress gulped down her pride and let Antony in on the situation. She loved her Persian carpets, she told him, but the Persians? Not so much. The troops Antony dispatched to Syria kicked Parthian ass, something he never succeeded in doing himself. Meanwhile the citizens of Rome—part of the western Mediterranean under Octavian's purview—were rioting because their leader had spent all the money in the public treasury. He was stoned and castigated in the Forum while attempting to explain this *faux pas* before being rescued at the last minute by Antony, who took him to his own house for medical treatment. History shows this was a serious blunder. Had Antony simply stood by and let the mob have its way the ancient world would have turned out very different. Despite this act of kindness Octavian continued to undermine Antony at every opportunity.

Antony and Cleopatra. This really was a love story. Having reached still another peace treaty with Octavian in spring 37 BCE and reaffirmed their division of the Roman world, Antony left for Syria with his army to deal with the Parthians, who continued to stir up trouble and gaze menacingly toward Egypt. A decisive victory would add to his eastern holdings, revitalize his popularity in Rome, and give him the political upper hand over Octavian whose word was unreliable. Conquering Parthia would also secure Egypt's borders, benefiting both Mistress and him. From Greece he sent Octavia and the children back to the safety of Rome. He never saw them again.

That autumn Mistress received a message from Antony asking her to meet him in Antioch, Syria's capital. There would be no games this time, no role-playing, no stage sets, perfumed sails, no extravagant banquets; in other words no superfluous political foreplay. Their goal was in sight, and each knew the stakes. Having not seen Antony in nearly four years Mistress played her hole card: she took along the children, whom Antony then acknowledged as his. Some say they married in Antioch, and this is written in the history books, but I have no recollection of it. There would have been no logical reason. Antony was already married to a Roman citizen. Foreigners lacked legal standing under Roman law even if married to a citizen of Rome, meaning Mistress' situation there would always be that of a concubine, never a wife. Egypt didn't require the queen to have a husband, just a male co-regent. For three hundred years of Ptolemaic tradition this personage had been a blood relative, although incestuous unions were never a requirement either. These marriages had often pro-duced progeny, but not always. Mistress relationships with her younger brothers had been chaste, and the light-hearted citizens of Alexandria much preferred Antony to anyone else as consort of their queen. Whether they were married to each other, to some-one else, or to nobody was irrelevant. And whether this other person was Egyptian or foreign, a consort without ruling authority or the queen's co-regent, was irrelevant too. General C and Antony had both served as Mistress' consorts, but her co-regents and legal husbands had been her younger brothers.

When Mistress and Antony eventually split sheets at Antioch—she to return to Alexandria, he to march with his army into Parthian territory—she was again pregnant. His war went badly; this time Parthia kicked Roman ass. Antony, once considered a brilliant strategist, had made some mistakes, like leaving his siege equipment behind to gain speed and not counting on an enemy skilled in guerrilla warfare. His allies proved a detriment, either demurring when asked to join the fight or double-crossing him. One time he led his men into a haline swamp; on another occasion they were forced to cross a wintery landscape without shelter and proper clothing where many died of hypothermia or lost fingers and toes to frostbite. In a campaign estimated to take three years, he quit the field after just a few months and limped west to safety with the remnants of his army, setting up camp on the coast of what today is Lebanon. It was winter. Still underclothed, his men were also starving and had not been paid. He sent Mistress word to come quickly and to bring clothes and money.

Her departure from Alexandria was delayed. Mistress was still recovering from giving birth to Antony's latest son, plus it took time to mint coins, assemble a fleet, and gather the clothing and other supplies Antony requested. Agitated, he paced the shoreline, waited, and hit the amphora, staying drunk night and day. By the time she arrived his reputation as a general was ruined and a third of his foot soldiers and half his cavalry were dead. Twenty-four thousand men had died during the extended retreat from Syria alone. In Rome Octavian crowed and Mistress was pilloried for urging Antony to start a war so late in the year, still more evidence she must have bewitched him. In truth, Mistress never had a vote. The Parthian campaign was entirely Antony's idea. She would have been satisfied if Antony had simply reinforced Egypt's borders to discourage encroachment, a purely defensive strategy. The lives of Antony's men had been wasted.

Sensing a possible breach between Mistress and Antony, Octavia sent word that she was also arriving with fresh military reinforcements, clothing, horses, money, and gifts for Antony and his officers. He told her not to come. She sent a messenger asking what was she then to do with all this stuff now that she had reached Athens? Mistress, knowing Octavia was prettier and still vying for Antony's affection, started a campaign to win him over. Ever the actress she chose for this role a love-sick, submissive woman resigned to losing a man. Her immediate advantage was being in Antony's presence while her rival was stuck fuming long-distance from Athens. Mistress quit eating, feigning a broken heart. When Antony walked by she gave him lingering, loving looks, pulled up her knees to make herself appear small, and clutched one of us cats as might a distressed adolescent girl. She made herself seem helpless, weeping often in great heaving sobs, hands covering her face; if asked the reason she bent her head down and shook it sadly. She seldom spoke, indicating she intended not to bother Antony during this stressful time, tacit recognition of his agony about Parthia, and only wished to be near him. Her singular reason for coming was love, her only purpose to help. She would do anything for him; he had only to ask as one soul-mate to another.

Want the hard truth? Besides Antony the most

Octavia could lose was her pride and perhaps her social status in Rome. Their marriage had satisfied a mutual political convenience. She was a beautiful young woman who would easily find another wealthy husband and in doing so recover her place in society, perhaps even advance it as her brother had done three years before. Octavian's lineage was not impressive despite having been adopted by Caesar, but this was a situation easily fixed. On the same day his wife gave birth in 38 BCE he divorced her and married a wealthy woman named Livia, six months pregnant with her ex-husband's child, a move that rocketed him into the upper echelon of Roman society. And Octavia's pride? Pride was something you got over, like flu or an ingrown toenail. Mistress on the other hand stood to lose not only Antony but a country, a throne, a large chunk of the Mediterranean world's capital, a royal heritage, and godhood. With all this at stake, winning was her only option.

The strategy worked. Afraid Mistress might kill herself Antony ordered Octavia and her entourage back to Rome and dismissed any thought of reprising the Parthian campaign so he could stay with Mistress. She was thinner now, pale, and genuinely weak. Having vanquished her rival there was no longer a need for further acting. She smiled often, no longer wept, and started to eat again. To Antony's mostly illiterate troops it seemed a miracle. What a performance! A cultured audience observing these events at a Forum would have stood cheering, clapping, demanding one curtain call after another, and peppering the stage with roses. Mistress surely earned those nonexistent accolades, and we cats deserved credit too. What better prop for a sad little girl to clutch to her chest than a kitty cat?

While Antony sat on the beach feeling sorry for himself and juggling his women, the amphora his best friend, Octavian crushed Sextus Pompey's navy and bribed Lepidus' eighteen legions to join him. Antony was his last impediment to uniting Rome's holdings and forming an empire. Although Mistress recognized Antony's unremitting grudge against Parthia, she knew Octavian to be the real enemy of them both. Antony also held a grudge against Armenia's king and felt he should be punished for his lack of support against the Parthians. Antony needed his ego stoked, so in the spring he invaded and conquered Armenia, captured the king and his family, and paraded them triumphantly down Alexandria's Canopic Way in gold chains, as befitted their royal status. That was in autumn 34 BCE, and Mistress spared no expense. Triumphs were a Roman thing, not really part of Egyptian culture, but everybody loves a parade. Had this been Rome the king would have been beheaded, but in Alexandria he and his family were merely imprisoned. He would lose his head later for other reasons.

Mistress and Antony were living large. She was delighted to keep Antony in Alexandria and away from Octavia, and he was happy to stay. Hers was a far more sophisticated and entertaining city than Rome, its loose and easy lifestyle better suited to his interests and personality. He spoke Greek in the extravagant local dialect and preferred Greek attire to dressing as a Roman noble. Mistress and Antony hosted numerous banquets, events at which people drank themselves stupid and groped one another. As a cat you get used to such scenes and sleep through the chaos.

A frequent guest was Plancus, an adviser to Antony who regularly arrived drunk, painted blue from head to toe, and naked except for a fish tail. He then wriggled around on the floor imitating a sea nymph. That no one had ever actually seen a sea nymph did not diminish the entertainment value of Plancus' theater. Whether this was his only shtick I can't say; rather, I didn't notice. I lost interest after discovering his tail wasn't from a real fish and therefore inedible. Neither can I confirm that Plancus painted himself blue or some other color. As I might have mentioned, a cat's vision is monochromatic, and we see the world in different shades of gray. A detriment, you say? Hardly. Have you ever seen a blue or chartreuse mouse? We see what we need to see.

Mistress and Antony went so far as to form the Inimitable Livers Club. Any member by definition became an Inimitable Liver, although more likely it was the member's own liver that strived toward the inimitable simply by surviving the next banquet. This was life as high art. Mistress as Isis was perfectly cast. Her wealth aside, she was exotic, elegant, ethereal, and, of course, fertile. She stood beside Antony, her consort, a ready-made Dionysus: handsome and curly-haired, strong, brave, generous, dipsomaniacal, fun-loving. Their subjects could not get enough.

In not returning to Rome Antony made a tactical error. There he might have recruited an army and kept Octavian at bay. He could now afford it. He and Mistress controlled lands populated by tax-paying subjects lining the eastern Mediterranean. Looting Armenia's coffers had further enriched Antony's eastern dictatorship, and lounging around on thrones posing as Isis and Dionysus was lots better than life as common mortals. Each had a throne, and Mistress' children sat on smaller thrones of their own. In a fit of largess Antony bequeathed the children various kingdoms and cities and appointed them titular rulers.

The peace agreement between Antony and Octavian expired at the end of 33 BCE, and there was no chance it would be renewed. The two men openly detested each other. Antony was content with ruling just half the Roman world, but Octavian wanted all of it. A war of words echoed back and forth over the Mediterranean Sea, Octavian claiming in the Senate and in pamphlets that Antony was a whoring drunkard, the consort of a foreign harlot who had given away Roman property to his bastard children and abandoned his loyal wife. Antony was so pussy-whipped that he had been seen massaging his concubine's feet, a task fit only for a servant or slave and well beneath the dignity of a Roman man, particularly one claiming to be a god. Antony retaliated: his adversary derived from a lineage of rope makers and bakers and who knows what else; why, it would not be a surprise to learn there was African blood in his ancestry. Octavian was weak, sickly, a proven coward who ran from the battlefield instead of toward it. The only thing he valued was his own ass. Look out, Rome, if this is how you define a leader.

Such schoolyard invective is always puzzling to a cat, who rarely knows its heritage and sees no point in attempting to trace it. That time is better spent napping or watching a mouse hole. Humans and cats are merely the tangible products of history over which no individual has control. As the saying goes, you can't pick your parents. What difference does it make who might have been your daddy? And Mommy hit the streets after weaning you? Get a life.

Even before their treaty expired both sides had begun recruiting and training men, stockpiling equipment, and building ships in preparation for the inevitable armed showdown. Consensus narrowed to a decisive battle somewhere in Greece. Mistress and Antony had everything to gain or lose, as did Octavian. Mistress, devoid of illusions, opened her treasury to her consort.

In April 32 BCE Mistress and Antony voyaged to Samos. Antony had at his command nineteen legions and continued demanding funds and recruits from the kingdoms he and Mistress controlled. Meanwhile

Octavian had heavily taxed the citizens of Rome to fund the cost of his militarization, and they were rioting in the streets. Sure everyone gets pissed when a dictator raises his taxes, but in this case there was no reason for it. In other words even though the treaty had expired there was really no excuse to start a war, harsh words notwithstanding. But it was too late. The time had come when any excuse would do, and Antony soon presented one. From Athens, where he had gone with Mistress, he sent notice to Octavia in Rome that he had divorced her. Effective immediately, she and the children—some of whom were his—were to vacate his house. The children included those fathered by her first husband, some the offspring of Antony and Octavia, and a son of Fulvia's fathered by Antony. Octavia was devastated. Octavian was ecstatic knowing he and Antony were no longer brothers-in-law.

Between Romans and Egyptians was a long-standing mutual dislike and distrust. Antony's Roman advisers considered Mistress a liability in the looming conflict and asked him to send her back to Alexandria. He refused, and so did she, reminding everyone it was she who had bankrolled most of the operation to date and that she intended on sticking around to monitor her investment. The charming music of her voice turned harsh and shrewish. Used to having her own way she screamed at Antony's aides and advisers and even threatened to have them tortured or executed. Misogynistic Roman men found such behavior in women repellent and demeaning, and in avoiding her they distanced themselves from Antony. Plancus packed his blue paint and fish tail and deserted to Octavian taking Antony's battle plans with him. Other valuable advisers and officers joined him. The dissention and unease grew with passing time. Armies and navies are assembled for battle and aren't good at waiting.

Octavian was a coward and a weasel, but he was no dummy. At the end of October he made a brilliant political maneuver, taking advantage of Rome's abhorrence of still another civil war. He declared war on Mistress—not Antony, his fellow Roman— claiming she had already conquered Antony's eastern dictatorship by holding him under her thumb and that Rome and the rest of the western world he controlled would soon follow unless he took protective measures. The war he proposed was a foreign one. His case was convincing despite its transparency. At the end of the year the Senate stripped Antony of his powers, one of which was latitude to recruit in Roman territories. Not that it mattered. By this time his forces had already been recruited and if more were needed he would simply ignore the laws. What the ruling by an essentially toothless Senate achieved had been to make Octavian supreme dictator *de facto*. Now the only obstacle remaining was the war itself, which compared with the heated build-up proved almost anti-climactic.

To protect Egypt and hence his supply lines,

Antony began deploying forces along the coast of Greece from Actium south to Methoni. In early 31 BCE Agrippa, Octavian's admiral, arrived unexpectedly in the Ionian Sea with his fleet intent on disrupting Antony's lines of supply. With Antony's forces still in flux Octavian took the advantage, moving eighty thousand men into Greece and forcing Antony north.

Mistress' presence in Antony's camp was moot, now that war had been declared on her personally. However her behavior and consequently her unpopularity with Antony's men remained unchanged. To Roman soldiers a woman could never be the equal of a man. A woman was expected to keep quiet and take orders. This one shouted and cursed at them and delivered orders, and Antony did nothing to stop her.

Her value soon became apparent in other ways. Nationalism, racism, and plain misunderstandings begin to appear in Antony's polyglot forces, and only Mistress seemed able to soothe these issues. Not only had she brought money along to finance the war and pay the troops, she could speak directly with the commanders of the eastern forces unfamiliar with Greek and Latin, dismantling the camp's obstructive language barriers and smoothing over smoldering differences before they could ignite into open hostility. In fluent Armenian, Ethiopian, Median, and other tongues unknown by the Romans she reminded them that her and Antony's benign rule would end if Octavian won, that they were not fighting for

Rome but their own interests. Most eastern rulers were accustomed to strong queens. In contrast with the haughty Romans who believed all women should be subservient, they had no problem accepting her leadership.

We were now camped at Actium, the most northern coastal site in Greece still safely controlled by Antony. The charm Mistress had applied in her dealings with her own allies remained nowhere apparent in her dealings with Antony's advisers and officers. She became agitated in their presence, sometimes making sarcastic allusions or more often directly threatening them with torture or death. I noticed because I suffered with them. She was getting headaches, the kind in which the backlight is transformed to an aura, a numinous halo that pulses and spikes in the brain behind the eyes. The blinding pain made her testy and short-tempered, and the Romans openly provoked her patience by disregarding her suggestions and ignoring her orders.

The blockade had shifted to lockdown mode. Supplies from Egypt slowed to a trickle. I noticed immediately when the milk in my bowl was replaced with water and on seeing that a few strips of greasy jerky had been substituted for my usual breakfast of smoked Nile perch and leftover pork. When I complained one morning by giving Mistress a hard stare and refusing to eat, she walked over and boxed my ears. And it wasn't just me. The officers were complaining too, muttering in Mistress' presence when the wine began turning to vinegar and their rations were cut. With the port now inaccessible Antony conscripted local villagers to transport grain and other necessities over the mountains. Full amphorae were too heavy and bulky for a man to carry. Until now the anodyne effect of wine had made the heat and mosquitoes bearable, but now the troops were in a mutinous mood.

One event disrupted the peace. It had nothing to do with the Romans, and in fact served them with a rollicking distraction. Aten had left the tent for a stroll around the camp, unusual for a cat who seldom abandoned his silk pillow except to eat, shit, and cuddle with Mistress. However Mistress had not been feeling cuddly for several weeks. Even Antony was on her shit list for not intervening in policy disputes in her behalf. That made him equally testy because he wasn't getting any at night. Perhaps all this distressed Aten in some way, although I doubt it. He was far too selfish and indolent even for a cat. At any rate he said nothing to me about his reasons. The excursion was short-lived. His appearance in the Ethiopian section caused a sensation. Thousands of soldiers poured out of the tents as he sauntered past. They began jumping up and down in unison and chanting a strange phrase. Mistress, who spoke Ethiopian, later told Antony it meant "When luck appears, wealth follows close behind!"

Such distractions would have spooked an ordinary cat and sent it running for shelter, but there was a reason for Aten's seeming insouciance. He was born completely deaf, a condition common in white cats with blue eyes but not especially so in albinos. Our immediate family—Mistress, Iras, Charmion, and me—were aware of Aten's condition; the rest of the world doubtfully knew or cared. It was Aten's undoing. Suddenly a long black arm terminating in thin fingers reached out of the mob and snatched Aten from his path. Similar hands clutched knives, and one of these blades slit Aten from chin to anus. Others stripped off his white skin, which disappeared into the crowd. Still more vultures with digits instead of beaks descended on the carcass and plucked out its organs, its eyes and tongue; stripped tendon from bone, muscle from tendon; snapped disarticulated bones into pieces. Everything vanished, leaving behind just a small spot of blood on the ground. To these Ethiopians albinos brought luck and wealth; that is, ownership of their parts could induce such life-altering changes. Had Aten been human his fate would have been the same.

Mistress was distraught. She knew it was futile to punish Aten's murderers because of religious or cultural beliefs. Being pragmatic she also recognized that doing so would upend her rapport with the Ethiopian leadership, diminishing her stature and authority. The Romans viewed Ethiopians as pagans and barbarians. To them the incident was amusing, especially so because it upset Mistress, temporarily siphoning away the abuse she had heaped on them and forcing Antony into the unenviable position of comforting a strong woman momentarily rendered weak.

Four months into the blockade and with winter looming, Antony finally acted. Some advisers recommended confronting Octavian's forces on land despite being outnumbered. Others urged attacking his navy. Desertions had made neither a viable option. Short on sailors, Antony ordered eighty of Mistress' ships hauled ashore and burned to keep them out of Octavian's hands. Onto some of the remaining ships he crammed twenty thousand troops unaccustomed to fighting at sea. There were sixty vessels left, including the huge Egyptian flagship *Antonia* still loaded with treasure and now with Mistress and her entourage aboard. Octavian's vessels outnumbered ours nearly two to one. Our navy sailed out of the harbor to meet Octavian's with *Antonia* and the remainder of the Egyptian ships not transporting troops serving as rear guard.

I was below and saw little of the actual battle of Actium, such as it was. Following several shifts and feints, Octavian's fleet was separated, leaving a clear path south. Mistress ordered her admiral forward. *Antonia* hoisted her purple sails and shot through the breach. That she raised sails at all surprised Octavian's admirals who anticipated a conventional sea battle with the ships maneuvered by oars.

Antony's ship hoisted sails and quickly followed. When well away from the battle he approached *Antonia*, hove too, and with a couple of his men climbed aboard. So it was that we escaped to Alexandria but lost the battle—and the war—to Octavian. Without their leader Antony's sailors and soldiers surrendered. Why had Antony, so brave in all respects and with a sterling reputation as a general, deserted his men in battle? No one knew. That he bore a terrible guilt was obvious. Aboard ship he and Mistress didn't speak, and it was only at the urging of Iras and Charmion, who acted as go-betweens, was the chilly silence finally broken and they agreed once again to sleep in the same bed.

6

Antony was put ashore in Libya where he had stationed four legions. The rest of us continued to Alexandria where *Antonia* entered the great harbor and Mistress staged a show from the decks signaling triumph, but the citizens already knew the truth. Her stature suddenly diminished, her authority crumbling, and an uprising imminent she went on the offensive, arresting and murdering her adversaries and confiscating their wealth. She knew Octavian would soon show up on the palace doorstep demanding an accounting. At best she might buy back her throne and be pardoned; at worst she would be paraded through Rome in Octavian's triumph and then publicly beheaded. Thousands of Alexandria's citizens died in her purge.

She used the funds to begin equipping a new army and navy. She called on former allies to join her in repelling Octavian's forces and found few takers. In desperation she planned to escape with Caesarian to a land beyond Octavian's reach, maybe India where her wealth could still buy them a good life. Or perhaps she and Antony and their children could sail to Spain or one of Rome's other northern outposts, bribe the Roman troops posted there to join them, and start a new colony of their own. She was flailing now, but that's what desperate people do. Despite the tenuous circumstances she remained confident and assured. Given the tiniest opening her intention, was to survive and do it in style. We absorbed her positive attitude. Whatever path she chose Iras, Charmion, and I would be with her. Beneath the skin we were tough. Mistress had already survived banishment to the desert, uncountable attempts on her life, and shown herself capable of imprisoning and murdering rivals. Iras and Charmion were slaves born of slaves; I was the offspring of strays.

It was Antony who had weakened, arriving in Alexandria drowning in guilt and self-loathing. He went immediately into hermit mode. He ordered a tiny island with a hut to be built in Alexandria's harbor, connected to the city by a narrow causeway. There he stayed in isolation after announcing that he was now in exile. From where he didn't say, but presumably Alexandria. He could never return to Rome. The Senate had effectively exiled him before the battle of Actium. On learning his Libyan troops had defected to Octavian he had attempted suicide, but companions intervened. Exile was fleeting. Pointing out that in case he hadn't noticed his hut was lacking good food and wine, not to mention a sensible place to shit, Mistress coaxed him back into her bed. She was now the strength of the partnership.

Antony soon recovered and they were again staging banquets and festivals, this time for the entire city. She told the citizens that no matter what might happen to her and Antony, her sixteen-year-old son Ptolemy XV (Caesarian) was ready to assume the throne and that Antony's and Fulvia's son Antyllus, a year younger, was prepared to assist him. Both boys then enlisted in the army as a show of faith. What I remember is being grateful for any return to normalcy, specifically a chance to reprise the good life underneath a banquet table instead of living in military camps. Even better, I was now the only palace cat, which meant more food and attention. No more sharing with slovenly butthole brothers.

Negotiations with Octavian commenced. Mistress was distressed once again, pacing the floor of her boudoir, sitting nervously at her dressing table, that one leg crossed and the foot bouncing up and down as if tied to a string and controlled by a puppet-master. In a sense it was, Octavian orchestrating the strings. She and Antony discussed everything, but Antony was mostly there to listen. He was never much of a politician or negotiator. Octavian had always been far shrewder, monopolizing their mutual insight into seeing ahead several steps. Mistress was his equal but operating at a disadvantage. All her life Egypt had been a protectorate of Rome; independence was impossible.

Egypt was too wealthy, and Octavian would never consider it. Her first choice was to remain on her throne, but was this negotiable? She was willing to abdicate if Caesarian were elevated to her place. After that? She would offer to abdicate and allow herself to be captured, paraded through Rome in Octavian's triumph, and even executed afterward if Egypt could keep its protectorate status under Caesarian. As for Antony he suggested being pardoned and permitted to live in Alexandria—or even Athens—as a private citizen.

The problem was that none of these propositions could be offered from a position of strength. If you don't have the other party by the balls the best you can hope for is to have each other by the balls so if one squeezes the other can squeeze back. In negotiating theory it's called a stalemate. That wasn't the case here. Octavian had his rivals by the balls including (figuratively) Mistress; they in turn stood facing Octavian empty-handed. Put simply, they had no bargaining power. Think about it. Why would someone of Octavian's known personality and history let Antony and Mistress live? Octavian was not only ruthless he was vengeful. He wanted them gone. Furthermore Caesarian was the great Julius Caesar's only son and therefore a potential future rival despite not being a Roman citizen. As anyone knows, rules can be changed. No, Caesarian was toast.

Octavian answered Mistress' proposals but not Antony's. He said he'd consider hers if she exiled or executed Antony, knowing neither would happen. They tried bribing him. He kept the bribes and turned down their requests. This was Octavian being Octavian.

Mistress and Antony disbanded the Inimitable Livers and founded a new organization based as before on extravagant consumption of all things edible and inedible. They named it the Companions to the Death Society. Mistress fast-tracked construction of a two-storey mausoleum for herself beside the temple of Isis, making certain it had a spectacular ocean view. A person needs that after she's dead. I should muffle my sarcasm. Views never did much for me, but I was going to be with her if the embalmers followed tradition. Antony? Who knew? Roman soldiers weren't especially religious. Other than claiming to share a godship with Dionysus and being descended from Hercules, what Antony mainly worshipped was wine and pussy. Surely there must be a place for both in the netherworld, assuming Antony gained entrance.

The parties continued while Mistress' empire collapsed around her. Ever hopeful of assuaging Octavian, she bribed and murdered minor Roman officials and military officers as necessary, to no avail. Some of Octavian's advance forces came ashore outside Alexandria where Antony, his courage restored and adrenaline surging, rode out with a few cavalry troops to meet them. He prevailed and sent a message to Octavian challenging him to single combat; to no one's surprise Octavian demurred having not overcome his distaste and fear of anyone approaching with a sharp object in hand.

Octavian's forces marched to the city gates and camped there; meanwhile his fleet bobbed in the harbor awaiting orders. On the night of 31 July 30 BCE Antony ate dinner and planned his attack. Early the next morning his depauperate infantry assumed posts outside the gates while his depleted navy rowed out to meet Octavian's—and defected. Next to desert was what remained of his cavalry.

Antony returned to the palace and upbraided Mistress for betraying him, accusing her of throwing her lot with Octavian, which she hadn't done. Some historians claim otherwise, but they're wrong. Although afraid for her life, she still loved Antony and would never have betrayed him. And she was too smart to succumb to any tricks, lies, and false flattery coming from Octavian's mouth. She was his equal at games of intrigue; it was Antony who was guileless. I know because I was present during those last days and nights. Iras and Charmion were too, and although their words and thoughts are lost forever, history has mine.

She knew the futility of trying to reason with Antony in his enraged, paranoid state. She left him and ran to the mausoleum where her jewelry and cash had been stored along with a good supply of firewood. If challenged she would immolate the building and herself with it. Confronting Octavian's well-known greed was the final card she held. She knew he was behind in paying his military and needed funds badly. The last thing he wanted was to see all that wealth disappear. Now locked in the mausoleum she sent a messenger to Antony telling him she had killed herself.

Antony was emotionally destroyed at the news. His troops and sailors had abandoned him; now the love of his life had deserted him too and was dead. It was over. Antony ordered his servant Eros to kill him, but Eros, ever loyal, shoved his sword under his own rib cage instead and died at his master's feet. Antony then unsheathed his sword and thrust it between his ribs but botched the job, somehow ending up with a painful abdominal wound instead of puncturing a vital organ or severing an artery. He begged his remaining companions to kill him, but instead they ran terrified from the room.

From inside the mausoleum, Mistress was attracted to the second-floor window by commotion below and peeked out. Seeing she was alive pushed the crowd into a frenzy. They shouted that Antony was not yet dead. She immediately dispatched servants to bring him to her. Charmion threw down a stout rope, the end of which was secured around Antony's chest just under the armpits. History then has Mistress, Iris, and Charmion together hoisting Antony up those two storeys and pulling him inside through the window, which is ridiculous. Antony was dead weight. He was also screaming and writhing in pain, which would have made the task even more demanding. The three women barricaded inside were barely five feet tall and a hundred pounds. I witnessed the entire event. They couldn't possibly have accomplished what was claimed.

The mausoleum was still under construction, and a crew of roofers had begun setting up the day before. Some bystanders fetched a wide ladder made specifically to bear the weight of men carrying heavy roofing materials and leaned it against the building. A burly man from the crowd shouldered Antony and carried him nearly to the top, close enough to push his head and shoulders through the opening, at which point the women pulled him inside.

They dragged Antony to a couch. Our grieving Mistress went at once into traditional mourning, smearing his blood on her face, pounding and scratching her chest, and calling him cherished husband and master. He waved his hand weakly as a sign for her to be quiet and asked for wine. He gave her advice about how to act when Octavian or his emissary came calling, to listen, and make the best deal possible for herself. He told her not to feel sorry for him, that he had died as befits a Roman soldier and no one could expect more. Remember instead his victories and honors. He then drank some wine and died in Mistress' arms. It was a tragic but appropriate end. Cats don't cry, although that moment was as close as this cat came. But the worst was yet to come.

Following Antony's suicide attempt one of his men had picked up the blood-covered sword and given it to Octavian, who took it into his tent and wept in front of his aides, false tears to be sure. Poor Antony, he intoned, brave but wayward comrade, fellow general, ex-brother-in-law. . . What a sad end to so promising a career. They could have ruled the world together had he only listened to reason. He stepped outside, dried his eyes, and read aloud some of their correspondence from years past, emphasizing passages proving what a true shithead and rascal Antony had been, penning insults and falsehoods that he Octavian had been willing to keep secret if not for this last fiasco. But now the truth was out. History would remember Antony for the drunken, whoring, roguish bastard he was. Octavian later burned those letters containing contradictory passages.

With Antony and his forces neutralized, Mistress and Caesarian were the last obstacles to absolute control of Egypt's fabulous wealth. The country's annual grain production alone was sufficient to satisfy Rome's needs and its own with enough of the bounty left over for profitable export elsewhere. The citizens would never again face food shortages and starvation. Civil unrest in the streets would end; the Senate would be in his pocket. Octavian could now satisfy all his debts, murder his remaining enemies with impunity, and appoint himself undisputed dictator of the entire Mediterranean world. Nothing and nobody stood in his way.

While Alexandria writhed in turmoil, Mistress sent Caesarian up the Nile along with his tutor, several bodyguards, and sufficient wealth to sustain them. The plan was for him to travel to India where he might live out his days in peace. This was not to be. As Egypt collapsed, Octavian's men tracked them down. Caesarian was returned to Alexandria where he was tortured and then murdered. Antony's son Antyllus had sought refuge in a temple. He was betrayed by his tutor, dragged into the street, and beheaded. Antony and Mistress' three children were later spared and sent to Rome where Antony's ex-wife Octavia raised them to adulthood. The daughter was married off to the regent of Mauretania, today's Algeria. The fate of the sons is unknown; some believe they accompanied their sister to her new kingdom.

For the present, Octavian desired two things. He wanted Mistress alive to display in his coming triumph, and he needed to grab the treasures stashed in her mausoleum before she could destroy them. To sweet-talk her he dispatched an emissary named Proculeius, a former friend and associate of Antony's. On his deathbed Antony had predicted this and advised Mistress to trust him, but when Proculeius arrived she refused to unbolt the door. Antony, she knew, was too trusting and easily duped, even at the end of his life. She trusted no one and carried a dagger to use on herself if necessary.

Proculeius went away and returned with Gallus, who a few days earlier had marched to the outskirts of Alexandria at the head of Antony's perfidious Libyan troops. He was a poet and scholar and Octavian had thought that perhaps Mistress might find his words and their delivery more appealing. She told him she had no intention of surrendering, but she threw back the bolt and the two negotiated at length in the doorway. Meanwhile Proculeius and two servants climbed the ladder still propped against the outside wall and climbed quietly through the window. Iras and Charmion yelled a warning to Mistress, but Proculeius overpowered her. He took away the dagger and searched her for poisons. He advised her gently to allow Octavian to prove his kindness instead of killing herself. He was actually a soft-hearted man who desired only her comfort and safety, not her death. Octavian's men then collected all sharp objects in the room, made an uneventful search for poisons, confiscated the treasure, and posted a servant to guard the door. His orders were to keep Mistress comfortable but closely monitor activities in the room. And at all costs see that she didn't kill herself.

Mistress spent the next two days washing Antony's body and rubbing it with spices. She screamed in grief, beat and clawed herself, and violently pulled her hair. Octavian granted her permission to bury her lover and attend his funeral. Afterward she became feverish from the self-inflicted scratches on her chest. This was good. She stopped eating, hoping to die. When Octavian heard of this he threatened to kill her children. She promptly abandoned the starvation as suicide plan.

Octavian held an assembly in the gymnasium, where he assured Alexandria's citizens he had no intention of harming them or disrupting their lives. In this he was sincere. You don't compromise the economy of such a rich prize as Egypt, damage its exquisite culture, and possibly incite the populace to rise against you. That would be stupid, especially with a disgruntled military force that still had not been paid. A kindly, peaceful approach was the perfect strategy. Octavian was one of history's greatest scoundrels and masters of sophistry, but an unerring ability to balance generosity and punishment accounts largely for his success. His standard approach: take the clearest path to a desired result using whatever means get you there most efficiently.

Mistress asked to meet with Octavian and then dressed in her finest linens and silks. He entered the room looking embarrassed and uncomfortable, maybe a little queasy, although a lifetime of stomach problems could have been the source. Mistress lay on her couch in a glamorous pose, purposely appearing wan and weak. Charmion had applied her makeup with just this cunning intent. Vulnerability and grace make an unmatchable combination.

She greeted him with a tired smile and addressed him as master and Caesar. Beside her was a stack of letters written to her by General C. She reiterated her love of Octavian's adoptive father and began to read aloud the glowing accounts of their relationship, hoping to gain a tenuous bond. Her performance was flawless. Unfortunately the situation rendered it awkward and compromising. Having not come from nobility Octavian was poorly educated. He neither spoke nor understood Greek. Every passage Mistress read was then repeated in Latin for his benefit by a laconic translator apparently selected without thought from among his field officers. The man's voice was guttural and uncouth, his diction and grammar uneducated.

Mistress' soft musical voice, reinforced by the gestures of an accomplished actress, were literally lost in translation. Her other option—reading the words directly in her own accented Latin—would have lessened their effect. Certainly Greek is the more supple language. She had not counted on the translator. If Octavian was moved he gave no outward sign. It seemed to me, lying on the couch beside General C's correspondence, that he barely paid attention. He was restless, fidgeting and periodically glancing around the room as if wishing Mistress' act and the rest of the interview would end. When it did he stood, assured her not to worry, and left.

Octavian was already posting the ships and troops he would leave in charge of the country and preparing the bulk of the deployment for departure to Rome. He would be pulling anchor in a few days accompanied by Mistress and her entourage, including her three children by Antony. She was granted a last trip to Antony's tomb, which she made by litter. Iras and Charmion went too. There she fell on her knees and wept. She accepted that her own death was now inevitable and begged Antony to appeal to the gods so their future together in the netherworld might be assured. He had been her life, her love.

Back at the mausoleum she bathed, ate a meal,

and dressed in her royal robes. Earlier a basket of figs had been delivered. The guards searched it and finding nothing unusual let it pass. Some historians say an "asp" was concealed among the fruits, that Mistress had planned it to be there, and that she stuck her hand under the lid and allowed it to bite her. Others claim she took out the snake and held it against her chest, where it bit her. In either case, death was from snakebite.

I was there as always, and this didn't happen. The so-called "asp" of ancient times is the Egyptian cobra, and these are large snakes. A medium-sized specimen is five feet long, an exceptionally large one twice that. A venomous reptile this size would be difficult to stuff into a basket of figs unless the basket is very large, and equally unlikely to lie quietly while the basket was carried around and passed from hand to hand. Believing the guards pawed through a basket of any size without discovering a big snake is incredulous. Mistress knew from her experiments that death from a cobra bite is not necessarily fatal but always painful, and that death, if it occurs, is slow. She also knew that a cobra releases all its venom in a single bite. Unless several snakes were to be smuggled in Iris and Charmion would have no way of joining her in mutual suicide. In fact, there was no snake.

Octavian's men had thoroughly searched the mausoleum for poisons and not found any. Again, I was there and watched them rummage clumsily through the closets filled with clothes, shoes, jewelry, and other belongings needed by three women confined together in a single large room. Where they didn't look was in the makeup kit. Egyptian men sometimes wore makeup, a practice demeaned as effeminate in Rome. The men who searched our quarters were Romans unused to examining female accoutrements. Even had they looked the poisons tinted with vegetable dyes would have remained hidden in plain sight. Mistress and her accomplices planned well.

After dressing, Mistress sent a letter to Octavian asking that she be buried with Antony. Suspecting suicide he immediately sent messengers to the mausoleum, but too late. Mistress lay dead on her couch attired as the queen of Egypt, and Iras lay dead on the floor beside her. Charmion could barely stand and was adjusting the diadem on Mistress' head just as Octavian's men burst in. "A fine deed this, Charmion!" one of them shouted. She replied, "It is indeed most fine, and befitting the descendant of so many kings." After speaking these words she too died and crumpled to the floor. The poison, which was oral, had worked quickly. It represented the culmination of many experiments. No prisoner administered this concoction had survived; all succumbed within minutes. Its composition was never discovered.

I lay beside Mistress unnoticed in the turmoil, but I was dying too. Before reaching for the diadem, Charmion rubbed the poison on her fingertip and induced me lick it off. The flavor was unfamiliar, although not unpleasant. As a strict carnivore it was not what I would have associated with food and more likely had been mixed to resemble something the noble rich considered a treat.

Antony's body had been interred without embalming, but Octavian honored the final request Mistress had made. She was embalmed according to Egyptian tradition and her mummy entombed with Antony, as were the bodies of Iras and Charmion. As the royal cat I was also embalmed and my body placed beside theirs. I was to be taken along for the ride, presumably to the afterlife. Cats aren't notably religious and maybe this is why I never got there; whether they made it I can't say. Somewhere on the journey we parted company but if you want my opinion I don't think anybody ever arrives. I've come to believe that when you're dead that's it. Lie there and decay, enjoying what remains of your molecules while they're connected, which won't be for long.

They say the tomb of Antony and Mistress is lost in time, that it lies buried under mud and twenty feet of water somewhere on the floor of Alexandria's harbor. Lost? Hardly. I was there, remember, and I know exactly where it is.

7

"That was fascinating," I said to Jinx. "So now tell me your story." Jinx turned on his deck chair and rolled onto his back, a maneuver Lucia once considered cute. When Jinx first came to live with us she thought this behavior was an invitation to rub his belly. We soon learned it was actually an excuse for him to scratch and bite us without expending the energy of getting to his feet. Jinx is friendly but not cuddly. He doesn't appreciate belly rubs. He also doesn't like being picked up or held, and if you do either he immediately struggles to be set down. That he might vaguely resemble a sleek stuffed animal is illusion. He's fifteen pounds of muscle and restrained havoc, an independent felid who enjoys hanging out with his humans but prefers doing so at a distance. Play touchy-feely at your risk.

Details of our mutual acquisition isn't much of a story but needs telling to kind of set the stage. Cats can be "adopted" from any number of sources, but we went to Cat Depot, a large clean facility a few miles away in Bradenton on the mainland where perhaps a hundred adolescent and adult cats live together in large walk-in cages. Prospective owners can sit on chairs in any cage they choose and interact with the incarcerated cats. After observing them—and they you—certain individuals stand out and you then approach these few as a test of their responses. Some of the cats have known pasts; others were given to the center without accompanying background information. As with people, personalities and idiosyncrasies of cats are partly genetic and partly shaped by experience. Strays taken off the streets can be nervous and suspicious. Those formerly a beloved pet are often the calmest and friendliest and more likely to be good lap cats, although some of them end up in shelters because they were not good pets. In either case a single interview reveals a little about them but not a lot. Some acclimate quickly to a new environment; with others the process is slow, and still others are too emotionally damaged to ever adjust. There's never a guarantee.

We've had many cats over the years, most of which lived into old age. Lucia has a mild allergy to them but still wanted one. Our lives felt slightly empty without a pet, and we agreed a dog would be too much trouble in a suburban neighborhood. A dog has to be walked and its turds collected in a plastic bag. Dogs bark and annoy the neighbors. Safety issues arise when they bite people and other dogs. They stink if not bathed regularly, and they track sand and other detritus into the house. Cats are quiet. They don't need human supervision, and they wash themselves. So a cat it would be. Lucia wanted it for company and to fuss over. I needed one to snooze on my desk while I work and to sit with me on the couch while I watch football on TV.

We spent most of an afternoon in mutual interviews with numerous candidates at Cat Depot. There was a particularly friendly female gray tabby named Grace Kelly, but we had always preferred male cats and reluctantly told Ms. Kelly she didn't make the cut. It shamed us to admit the reason was gender bias. A black and white male obviously wanted to adopt us. He demonstrated this by hopping into Lucia's open handbag on the floor and refusing to get out. He was certainly a top candidate. The manager told us that every cat on the premises cost a hundred dollars, which included neutering and shots. Black cats were exceptions. They cost only seventy-five dollars because many people think they bring bad luck and refuse to adopt them. Some had lived at Cat Depot for years despite having nice dispositions. It was sad. So we decided to get a black one. I was already imprinted on black cats. My favorite cat of all time had been black, a big friendly tom I'd raised from a kitten in the 1960s and named Puddy Tat. I still remembered Puddy with great fondness. He was awesome.

Cat Depot housed dozens of black cats, fewer after we'd narrowed the possibilities to males. Lots of them seemed nice, then there was one who was barely noticeable. He sat by himself watching us. We picked him up. There was no biting or scratching, but he jumped off our laps immediately. He didn't run away or try to avoid us. He merely sat on the floor as if waiting for something to happen. He was calm and unusually self-assured, entirely nonplussed by the other cats or the humans walking around talking loudly. A volunteer at the shelter had named him Rhinestone. His history was blank except to note he was a stray brought in from the streets by Animal Control.

Lucia has a remarkable ability to look once at an animal and bestow on it the perfect name. When we started dating she owned a barking tree frog named Max. After getting to know Max I thought all barking tree frogs should be named that. When we moved to Florida she discovered a cockroach living in our storeroom. She named it Anthony, although it could just as well have been Antonia. (Archy of course was already taken.) No cockroach in my experience ever lives alone, and they mostly look alike. Not to worry, Lucia said. We'll just name them all Anthony, that way we won't have to know each one personally. I have to admit it keeps things simple.

This black cat we were interviewing sat on the floor and stared at us, then became bored as cats do and started to lick his front paws. Was he interviewing us? That was hard to tell because he closed his eyes and seemed to fall asleep while still sitting up. Dogs are open and obvious, so you always know with a dog. Cats are cryptic and aloof.

"He doesn't look like Rhinestone to me," Lucia said flatly. "Especially if he's going to be our new roommate. I just don't see myself living with a Rhinestone. I'm a diamond kind of girl."

"What does he look like?" I said.

"It's obvious he looks like Jinx," she said.

I didn't think it was obvious, but then I'm not an expert when it comes to naming animals. "Okay," I agreed. "He's Jinx." We paid the seventy-five bucks and took him home.

I mentioned to Jinx how he got his name, news he accepted with a yawn.

"Okay so you gave me a name, or rather Lucia did. Big deal. Being the typical scientist you're unfamiliar with good literature and basically helpless and ignorant outside your own field. I doubt you've read T. S. Eliot's short poem titled 'The Naming Of Cats.' It leads off his little compendium *Old Possum's Book Of Practical Cats*."

"No," I confessed. "That one got by me."

Jinx let this hole in my education slide without comment. "Evidently Eliot figured out something the rest of you haven't, specifically that a cat who lives with humans typically has three names. The first is a sobriquet, or family name. Jinx in my case. The second name is formal, oozing class and sophistication. A Show Time name. Eliot suggested several including Munkustrap, Quaxo, Coricopat, and Bombalurina. You obviously never considered giving me a second name, possibly because I'm an alley cat instead of a snooty purebred. For example a brown tabby in the American Shorthair division named Sol-Mer Sharif won the Cat Fanciers' Association Best of Show in 1995. In 2006 the winner was a Blue Persian named Jadon Comefly With Me of Kenkat. In 2012 a chocolate spotted Ocicat named Wild Rain Let's Dance of Dotdotdot took home the prize. But a former stray such as myself? Not a chance. What am I, chopped liver?"

I lit a cigar and set the lighter down on the table between us. "Poor baby," I said in my best whiny voice. "How about Laudable Malfeasant Propagator of Panhandling and Dumpster Diving? It seems to fit."

"Thanks. About what I'd expect from a philistine. Continuing with Eliot's poem, no human ever learns a cat's third name, just other cats. We address one another by means of telepathy using third names, which are kept strictly secret from humans. You're limited to giving and using just our first and second names. Way back in cat history before we started associating with you we had only a single name, which is now the third."

"So what's your secret name? I can keep a secret."

"Screw you. Good luck finding out."

"Your so-called 'secret' name might be a big deal to other cats but I couldn't care less. So don't tell me and see if I give a shit. I suppose it's like those street names hoodlums use to pass themselves off as cool. You know, Sweetgum, Britches, High-Life, T-Bone, Thumbs, 4-Stroke, Bugsy, Ghost. . . Do street cats go out of their way to be cool?"

"Hardly. In my case I'm cool either way, which you damn well know. That third name is just a cat I. D. I picked up after Mom weaned us behind some dumpsters. That was up the highway in St. Petersburg. I've always walked tall, holding my tail vertical. Other cats knew not to mess with me, not that we did a lot of fighting. You got that part right in your book about free-ranging cats. Kind of surprised me. You aren't as dumb as you look and act."

"Thanks—I think. I guess you like me."

"I wouldn't go that far. You two make convenient servants. The grub and living conditions here are passable, and hanging out with you hasn't proved excessively boring or irritating. At least not so far. Then of course I'm a cat and sleep about twenty hours out of every twenty-four. Getting down to it I'm probably not the one to ask how boredom should be defined."

"Okay," I said, "cut the sarcasm and wise guy act and tell me something new. For example Lucia and I don't know anything about your past before our meeting at Cat Depot. By then you were an adult. What was life like on the streets?'

"Well, I started life as a kitten."

"I figured that already, hairball."

"Now who's being sarcastic?"

"Cut it out and get on with the story; that is unless your life has been nothing but a long nap."

"As I said before, I'm an alley cat. I was born in an alley and lived in several others early on. There were five in my litter. I had two brothers and two sisters. We separated at weaning. Eventually we split for different parts of town and I never saw them again. Well maybe I did, but if I had I wouldn't have recognized them anyway. We cats don't clutter our minds with long-term memories of other cats except, in a historical context."

"What was Mom like?" I said.

"She was an orange tabby, thin and mangy. A stray, of course. Nothing to look at and extremely wary of humans. She was there to protect us, I suppose, but stray dogs and raccoons were the only danger. Other cats pretty much avoid kittens. Mom would nurse us, then disappear to hunt rodents or scrounge in a garbage can. She didn't say much."

This set me thinking. I had lots of questions about cats and now was the time ask them. "Yeah," I said, "but you're a helluva ratter. You've dragged in several since you've come to live here, much to Lucia's disgust. It's been my conclusion from studying cat biology that cats are born killers and nobody 'teaches' them hunting skills. What's your opinion?"

"First off, Lucia needs to suck it up. Those were trophies and should be admired, especially considering how carefully I arranged them on the tile in the foyer."

"Yes, what's more artful than a disemboweled rat carcass?" I said. "Especially when placed strategically in a pool of its dried blood and entrails and garnished with still-wriggling blowfly maggots. You forget who's always called to rat-disposal duty. Guess I should have mounted the heads and hung them on the wall, eh?"

"Actually that would be a nice touch. You really need to hire a decorator. Contrary to popular lore, mother cats don't 'teach' their kittens to hunt. That's a load of crap. Hunting comes naturally. I remember the last few weeks of my kittenhood very clearly, and Mom didn't 'teach' us diddly-squat. Even when kittens are young what humans call 'play' is really hunting behavior. Not 'practice' hunting as some of the 'experts' claim, but *real* hunting. That a prey animal isn't killed doesn't make their intent less real. Not every hunt by an adult results in a kill either. And because the object isn't necessarily edible at this stage in our development doesn't make it 'play' by default.

"Catching food is serious business, something you wouldn't know anything about seeing as how everything you eat comes packaged. You think we're cute when we chase a string in 'play,' but that's only because you're incapable of interpreting the world from our perspective. 'Survival skills' in your case is an oxymoron. It means being able to find the liquor store. All humankind is mostly hairless, slow, and ignorant of nature, not to mention graceless and ugly. Your claws are weak, your carnassial teeth dysfunctional, your senses of smell and hearing pathetic. You couldn't survive butt-naked outdoors for any length of time without dying of hypothermia or starvation. I'd be first to applaud if you—my very own personal human—managed to catch a stick of celery. Luckily your species learned to manufacture clothes and took up farming and ranching.

"Once my littermates and I were up and running around the alley, Mom started bringing us live mice that we quickly learned to kill and eat. However Mom wasn't 'teaching' us to hunt and kill or anything else. She had no 'motive' for doing what she did, not by any definition, conscious or unconscious. Taken at face value her behavior seems altruistic by putting our interests before hers: she'd caught a mouse and instead of eating it she gave it to us. But if you believe this you'd be wrong. In truth the driving factors were surging concentrations of maternal hormones timed to coincide with a critical point in our development, specifically the moment when we suddenly discovered that foods other than Mom's milk were interesting and digestible.

"Before and after this narrow time interval when a mother cat catches a mouse she eats it herself and to hell with her kittens. So Mom wasn't being unselfish at all. She was simply behaving as nature programmed her to be. New human mothers have surges in these same hormones, the difference being that because they form strong and permanent attachments to their offspring these maternal instincts can last a lifetime, even after the hormones that prompted them have attenuated.

"Maternal hormones in cats decline rapidly and soon return to pre-pregnancy concentrations after the kittens are weaned. We noticed right away. How could we not? Mom quit acting like a mom and couldn't give a rodent's rear end about us. Now able to forage on our own we weren't her responsibility anymore. I recall trying to beg a last suckle one afternoon as Mom was resting. She gave me a swat upside the head and turned her back to me. It wasn't a motherly rebuff either; this time her claws were out. I got the message. That night she brought home a mouse and ate it in front of us while we watched and drooled.

"But we got over it. Hunger does that. In cats, a mother's love goes only so far, then it's sayonara and see you around the dumpster, but don't expect hugs and kisses. I frankly doubt that I'll recognize you, and strange though it sounds now, I doubt you'll know who I am either. Seem cold and impersonal? It isn't. It's life.

"For about six months after weaning I stuck around the birth site scavenging in garbage cans and catching mice. Rats were still a little too big and intimidating. I needed to put on some size before tackling them.

"That mention of a kiss brought up an unpleasant memory. A group of humans used to come to the next alley over and feed the strays. I avoided the place if I could despite the free grub. It was always that dry stuff they call kibbles, and always a cheap discount brand, not that I'd have thumbed my nose at it back then. It's just that those people were truly weird. They called themselves Friends of Alley Cats or something similarly lame. I can't remember exactly. They showed up in a van, maybe a half-dozen or so old ladies, and jumped out yelling, 'Here kitty, kitty!

Here kitty, kitty. Mommy's here with your lunches!'

"Mommy's here? Can you believe it? And most of the dopey cats in the area came running. Problem is, lots of the cats I knew from over there disappeared. I mean permanently. They didn't come back. Sure we moved around, but it was strange to be here one day and gone the next and always from that alley where the free grub was handed out.

"One afternoon I took a stroll over there to check things out. I no sooner arrived than the van showed up and those same old ladies hopped out yelling 'Here kitty, kitty!' I hid behind a dumpster and waited to see what happened. It's been my experience that humans usually want or expect something from you. There's no free lunch. No cat is a math whiz, but I counted only four of the old biddies dishing out kibbles. The fifth had disappeared; the sixth seemed to be hiding in the van, but from what? From the cats, that's what. Another who seemed to be the leader was studying the cats now gathering in the alley and checking off sobriquets from a list on her clipboard. 'There's Raymond, and the calico over there is Mildred. They're always around. Ah, come here Gladys, the little sneak. I can see you behind those garbage cans. You can't hide from Mommy.' I wanted to puke. What kind of a dumb felid would fall for such drivel?

"I was fixated on the scene before me and not being vigilant. The old woman who I thought had disappeared sneaked up quietly behind me. She grabbed me suddenly and lifted me into the air. I had never before been touched by a human, and this first encounter wasn't pleasant. 'I got a newbie!' she yelled. That's when the last old lady, the one hiding in the van, came stumbling forward carrying a cage. I started to squirm but the hands gripped tighter. 'Calm down little dear,' she cooed. 'Oh you sweetie,' she said. Her face looked like a newly ploughed field, rouge and sweat gushing down the furrows. Then to my disbelief she kissed me right on the mouth. I squirmed harder. As she was lowering me toward the open cage door I struck out furiously and scratched her arms from shoulder to fingertips. For good measure I bit one of her hands. She yelped and dropped me, and I ran for my home alley."

"She kissed you on the *lips*?" I said.

"Yeah, she sure did. When I finally found shelter I licked my ass for nearly an hour just to get the taste out of my mouth. What a disgusting experience. But the venture had been educational. A week or so later a male stray called Barney who occasionally wandered through our alley showed up. He'd been one of the *desaparecidos* and a fine strapping tom in his day, but when I next saw him he was skinny and had no balls. Literally, no balls.

"He told me he'd been suckered into that free chow and actually become friendly with those old women, letting them pet him, even pick him up and cuddle him. Then one day when he wasn't paying attention they popped him into a cage and whisked him off to an animal shelter where some veterinary types zoned him out, stuck him with needles, wormed him, and cut off his nuts. After he recovered a human visiting the shelter adopted him and told him no more wandering around outdoors. From now on you eat kibbles and like them, and you shit only in kitty litter. And don't scratch the goddamn furniture. There were lots of odd rules strays don't have to follow or even know about. One day his 'owner' (Christ I hate that term) forgot to close the door. He split and found his way back. Cats have terrific homing instincts. No more kibbles for him, he said, from now on it was rodents and garbage and you shit where you please."

"Jesus, and everybody thinks they're doing strays a favor by taking them off the street," I said.

"Well someone forgot to ask the cats. To quote a nursery rhyme, not by the hair of your chinny-chin-chin," said Jinx. "What any cat wants is basically to be left the hell alone. Oh, and by the way, *don't ever* kiss me on the lips or I'll rip your own right off your face."

"No worries there, mouse breath," I said. "But tell me some more about life on the street. Down and dirty? Did you go hungry a lot?"

"It was freedom, my man, freedom. You did what you wanted when you wanted, and there weren't any rules."

"You pretty much have that here," I said, "and the food is better. Do we tell you how to behave, where to go at night, check who your friends are? Maybe a swat with a rolled-up newspaper when you scratch the furniture, that's about it, right?"

"Yeah, life here is pretty good, but that newspaper. . . I could get you busted for animal cruelty."

"That's only if I manage to hit you with it. So far you've been too quick. Anyway it's your word against mine, and you don't speak or know how to dial a phone."

"I could go to the neighbors and scream piteously outside their door and fake a limp."

"The neighbors are dog people, remember? I'll advise them to call Animal Control if you start bugging them."

Jinx seemed to abandon that idea. "About the furniture, what's your problem? Bunch of rags and sticks is all I see."

"Tell me," I said, "what's the appeal of all this clawing? I know you aren't marking your territory with scent glands in the paws for two reasons. First, cats have home ranges but don't have territories. Second, they also don't have 'scent glands' in their paws. And when we rub our cheeks against something no scent is transferred because cats don't have 'cheek glands' either. The most you're doing by scratching something is pulling off the old claw sheaths, which keeps the claws sharp for hunting. This doesn't 'sharpen' them as a fingernail file would; rather it allows them to *stay* sharp. I know this, so what's the point of trashing the furniture?"

"It feels good," Jinx said simply. "Speaking of which. . ." He started extending and retracting his claws and no doubt had designs on the deck chair's fabric, which is made of perforated plastic that looks superficially like cloth.

"Don't even think about it," I said as menacingly as I could. "This neighborhood has lots of trees. You're looking at some right now. Why don't you go scratch them instead? We paid for that furniture, and you're ruining it."

Jinx rolled onto his back and gave me a fetching upside-down look. He probably expected me to flash him a fish-eating grin and toss a compliment his way. He probably expected me to say, "Aw that's so cute" like Lucia does. Instead I frowned and glared at him, or tried to. However that glare turned out, it was the best I could manage in my condition. I could tell Jinx wasn't impressed.

"I do scratch trees," he said from upside-down. The phrase sounded different with his head in that position, backward or something. It came out "seert hctarcs od I." I was about to say as much when he rolled back over and continued: "When I'm outdoors and trees are handy, but when I'm indoors the furniture is more convenient, especially on rainy days."

"Careful," I said in my most chilling voice. "I could always return you to those kindly people at Cat Depot."

"I doubt if they'd take me back. Just what they need, another black cat nobody wants. Most humans know better than to adopt us. We're generally a pain in the ass, especially around Halloween when we start yowling from rooftops and scaring the shit out of little trick-or-treaters. Not to mention crossing the paths of as many people as possible, preferably when the light is dim and spooky."

"I noticed the pain in the ass part," I said. "Every day is Halloween since you moved in here, but back to life on the street, okay? Try to stay focused."

"You're advising *me* to stay focused?" Jinx went into a series of minor spasms accompanied by a sneezing fit, an episode so violent he had to sit up. I suppose that's what a cat does when it's laughing really hard. I'd never seen one laugh before. It was unnerving. He stopped after a few seconds and settled back in the chair.

"Of course I remember life on the street," Jinx said calmly, now composed. "Some of my best memories happened there. You mentioned the food. Incredible spreads! There's no smorgasbord anywhere like your average dumpster. Never know what to expect. Every garbage bag ripped open is a Christmas day feast. There was this dumpster in our alley outside a steak joint in St. Pete, and if I felt the urge for a steak dinner I sauntered over there after dark. The chef had a fierce temper, and when a customer sent back a steak because it was overcooked he threw it in the garbage. Then the waitress who'd brought it back got an earful like it had been her fault. Sometimes the new ones cried, but those with years of tossing them off the arm in that place just told him to go fuck himself. On a busy weekend night we cats ate so much steak we had belly aches for a couple of days. Got so we routinely turned down hamburger.

"When we got bored with steak there was a seafood place a few doors down also with its own dumpster. Most humans never learn to properly pick all the meat out of a lobster tail even with those ridiculous little forks, which by the way bear an uncanny resemblance to a pair of cat claws placed side by side. With a little practice a cat easily learns to scrape out the remaining meat. Then follows another belly ache (all that lemon butter) but what a meal. Which brings up a point I've been meaning to ask: why don't we ever have lobster?"

"Because it's too expensive. If I want lobster I eat out. I learned long ago how to clean out the tail meat, so no kitty bags. If you have a craving for lobster there's a seafood joint up the road a couple of miles. It probably has a dumpster in back so you should feel at home. You can arm-wrestle the squad of raccoons that hangs out there for leftovers." I leaned back and put my hands behind my head as a guy does when sitting in the catbird seat.

8

Jinx didn't take the bait but kept babbling on about the terrific dining city alleys make available to the discerning stray. "Of course breakfast consisted of last night's leftovers, although hanging around in back of a local breakfast joint could also be worthwhile. I had a soft spot for one in particular. It was a small operation with no dumpsters, just several uncovered garbage cans. There might as well have been signs on them saying hop right in and order one of the morning specials such as eggs over easy, your choice of ham or bacon. Lots of single women met there, which made it especially enticing."

"Hold on. You prefer women to men?" I must have sounded confused.

"No, it's their dining habits I prefer," Jinx said. "They eat less, meaning more is left on their plates. When women gather to ingest food they uncon-sciously make a point to act dainty around their peers. They don't think it's ladylike to eat everything served to them so invariably some food gets thrown away. Men on the other hand scarf even the crumbs then wipe up the runny egg yolk with a last piece of toast leaving nothing for a poor starving cat shivering outside. Now lunch? Lunch is different. Then you avoid those places that offer mainly 'chick food' because it consists of lots of salads covered in vinegar. A dog will eat a discarded salad, but then a stray dog will eat anything. We cats are persnickety. We're also strictly carnivorous unless truly down and out. Then we might lower ourselves to nibble some carbohydrates. But salads? We'd rather starve."

"What about, uh, 'natural foods' like birds and rodents? You haven't mentioned them. I'm curious because even a satiated cat still hunts, assuming there's something to hunt, and with all that food around there must have been lots of mice, rats, pigeons, sparrows, everyone sharing in the feast."

"Sure, there was fresh meat everywhere. You just had to know where to look. Once I grew up I started taking on rats. An adult rat can be quite the challenge, especially one that's had previous experience evading cats. A cornered rat comes right at you, then it's nature fang and claw. I loved it. I remember one in particular. He lived underneath the dumpster outside that steak restaurant and feasted on sirloin and prime rib and grew nearly to the size of a small stray cat.

"One night Barney and I managed to pin him against a wall away from the dumpster where he couldn't make a run for it. We were growling and yowling, the rat was screaming this high-pitched scream and all of us were thrashing around among the discarded newspapers and making a helluva fuss. The scrap got so loud the dishwashers could hear us, even with the usual racket of chefs yelling and pots and pans banging. The kitchen itself was steaming inside so the door was open to the alley. Barney and I eventually got the rat onto his back and killed him, but not before he bit us both pretty hard on our faces. See this scar?" He motioned with one of his paws to a streak of bare skin above his right eye where the hair had never grown back. "After it was over, Barney and I looked up and there were three or four guys standing on the steps wearing greasy aprons and smoking cigarettes. They'd witnessed the battle and started to cheer and clap. It was awesome! When you kill a rat everyone appreciates the effort."

"Did you eat it?" I said.

"Naw, we'd just chowed down on steak and weren't hungry. Cats, as you say, are born killers. Killing is what we do. What triggers us is simply the thrill of the hunt. Those do-gooders who make a vocation of feeding strays never understand that vaccinating and feeding us won't save wildlife, it just allows us to live longer so we can kill even more small animals over our now-extended lifetimes."

"I take it rats don't count," I said.

"Vermin never do," Jinx said. "Nobody objects to cats killing rodents or even birds often classified as vermin like English sparrows and pigeons. Nobody wants pigeons around. Ask any statue. The best meal of all is a litter of baby mice while they're still naked and pink and before their eyes open. What a treat!"

I said, "The problem cats have with conservationists is their general failure to distinguish noble species from vermin. If you could just learn to do this all would be well."

Jinx didn't reply, then started to wash himself. "Ain't going to happen," he said between licks on his hind leg. "Don't expect a cat to read a list of local Endangered Species and carry around a field guide to the birds. To us if it runs or flies it's game."

"Yeah I know about that. I wrote a book about cat behavior and biology, remember? You were there beside me on the desk usually lying with your head near my keyboard. Sometimes when you stretched you'd even do a little typing. I remember sssssssssss showing up on the screen, or if you were feeling especially literary it might be eeeeeeeeeee. But mostly you were copping zzzzzzzzzzzzs. And you spent lots of time sitting on whatever scientific paper I was reading or abstracting information from. Each time I put down an open book or a journal article beside the keyboard you immediately sat on it and didn't move until I yanked it out from underneath your hairy ass."

"Ah, and you claim to understand cat biology," Jinx said, his words coming at me with unusual clarity. On hearing this and glancing over and I could swear I saw him actually grinning out of the darkness. But the mouths of cats are fixed. A dog can manipulate its lips into a sort of grin, but not a cat. I must have imagined it.

"What humankind has never known until now— right this minute—is that we cats absorb human knowledge through our anuses. You're the first of your species to hear about it, so take a deep breath and feel special." As Jinx said this he leaned against the back of his chair as a cat might when sitting in the catbird seat.

I was stunned. Cats absorb written knowledge through their anuses? The notion seemed as incredible as it was unlikely, but who was I to argue. All great breakthroughs in science are initially discounted by the mainstream, so why not this one?

"Okay," I said. "I'm skeptical. Let's see some proof."

Jinx immediately presented synopses from import-ant discoveries in cat biology as outlined in my book. He recalled the article published by British scien-tists in 2010 in which they calculated the average daily energy requirement of adult cats, also citing the standard allometric equation they used to derive it. He knew the physiological reasons why cats fed moist diets never need to drink water and cited pub-lished work demonstrating that carbohydrates have no useful function in a felid diet and can even be harmful. He knew the recent findings in cat genomics I had summarized, that territoriality in domestic cats is a fallacious concept, and that cats aren't social as commonly believed but rather the opposite. I'd set down this information and much more and he knew it as intimately as if he had written it himself. By the time he finished talking my hands were trembling so much I could barely top off my snifter of rum and light another doobie.

"Wow," was all I could manage. "Being a cat you would obviously know about the social aspect having experienced it firsthand; that is, catting around and such. So let me confirm or reject some points that remain contentious among the experts. Most believe cats have territories. I don't because a territory is defined as a defended area. I contend that cats have home ranges, meaning areas in which they live and travel through. Am I right?"

"Yup. We cats don't defend specific areas against other cats, and we travel through each other's home ranges with impunity. Nobody cares; it's just space. Next you're going to ask if we're social creatures, aren't you? Don't answer. We aren't. We're *asocial*. We prefer to avoid each other except during mating season. The reason why you sometimes see bunches of stray cats is because they've gathered around a source of food: a dumpster, some garbage cans, people handing out kibbles. We're there for the free grub, not to visit each other. We aren't dogs for chrissakes. And when a female is in heat we males stand around waiting our turns. We don't fight over her. That's also urban myth. And something else: after a female has been laid and the male pulls out, she turns into a tigress, attacking him fiercely. Nobody knows why except that the male cat penis is covered in tiny spines and a retracting pecker probably hurts like hell. Anyway lots of scratches on the faces of old toms aren't from fighting other toms. Ask one what happened to his face and he'll likely say the battle scars came from ungrateful females. Go figure."

"I'm confused about something else," I said. "Did you recount Annipe's tale directly from her databank of recollections via the Cat Memory Channel or did you read Egyptology in some textbook and invent it?"

"Annipe's tale is real enough, and I retold it to you as it happened. She beamed it directly to me. Of course I've also absorbed some Egyptology and a lot of other stuff, none of which altered Annipe's experiences. In my wandering days I set out to see the world from the vantage point of different alleys, trying new foods, chasing pussy, hunting birds and rodents. . . Cats aren't territorial. We go where we want, taking up temporary residence here and there. I lived for a time in an alley outside a college dorm and cafeteria. That might have been the most boring dumpster I ever frequented. Most nights there was nothing except pizza crusts and crumbs of marijuana brownies. At least you could keep a buzz going.

"There were other advantages like discarded books and the semi-literate papers written by students. If the food was piss-poor at least there was knowledge for the absorbing while you dined. We cats don't have to page through books and documents. Humans invented pages because they have fingers to turn them. Cat paws aren't very effective at this. However we can sit on top of a book with our anuses pressed against it and drill sequentially through from start to finish, metaphorically of course. The information it contains is transmitted directly from asshole to brain. Think of it as anal-brain circuitry, a biological precursor of the analog computer.

"Living around that dumpster was where I met Homer. He was a homeless human and I was a so-called homeless cat, so we had a natural connection. I was perfectly content with my situation. Homer, in contrast, had this load of guilt he was toting around that sometimes got him down and induced a hard case of the sorries. Then he'd sit with a wall propping up his back drinking cheap dago red from a bottle and bitching how life is a shit sandwich. Other than yourself, Homer was the only human I've ever talked to, and I have to tell you that he was really, really fucked up or we could have never connected.

I said, "Thanks. . . I think. I mean that sarcastically, as in thanks a lot, you bastard, for reminding me how fucked up I am, not whether I'm unsure if I actually said thanks or that I'm thanking you because I think it. Maybe I think it, maybe not, but I did say it, right? Well, hell. . . " I took another pull on the doobie and cleared the palate with a sip of rum.

Jinx sat staring at me from his chair and for a full minute didn't speak. I guess he was thinking, although with cats it's hard to tell. Then he said, "I'll repeat: Homer was truly fucked up or we'd have never

connected. Not that you're fucked up, of course."
Then I swear he grinned again.

"I got to know Homer pretty well," Jinx continued, now that this random train wreck of a conversation had been set upright at least temporarily. "He was a former adjunct biology professor at the university, one of those untenured jobs without benefits in which you're paid a flat fee to teach a course. The faculty tosses you crumbs, assigning you teach the classes no one else wants to teach but are required in the degree program. If you're offered only one or two classes a semester the pay isn't enough to live on. Homer was also trying to finish his doctorate in the same department, and when he complained about his situation they kicked him out. His research had focused on the biology and behavior of urban stray cats. Without knowing it I'd been one of his subjects. I'd noticed him lurking around the alleys for a couple of years collecting field data, a heavily bearded guy with long scraggly hair and dressed in dirty shorts, tees, and flip-flops. He was always carrying a notebook and writing down stuff.

"I formally met Homer one hot summer dawn after returning to the abandoned car where I'd been crashing and anticipating a peaceful snooze. I'd been up all night foraging and fucking and a few winks were on the agenda. But there was Homer sacked out on the front seat—in fact the only seat, the one in the back having been set afire a few years before by another homeless guy.

"I meowed a couple of times and pawed at Homer's face trying to convey that this was my personal abandoned car and he was squatting. He finally opened his eyes and said, 'Oh, hi #77. Wassup? That's right, I'm in your bed. Got that in my notebook and forgot. Sorry.' We weren't actually conversing at that moment but he knew what I wanted and slid over to make a little space. I was beat and figured what the hell. I accepted his offer and curled up next to him. He smelled awful, a combination of dago red, halitosis, stale cigarettes, and that peculiar body odor certain unwashed humans retain that can clear even a roomful of vagrants. Probably what Annipe meant when referring to Antony's smell. It took a few days but eventually I quit noticing.

"We slept all day and in the evening got up to take a piss, me in a patch of dirt beside a broken-down fence, Homer against a wall. Then it was time to eat. Homer knew the alleys and placement of dumpsters as well as us cats, having followed us for many months. That evening he followed me to behind the steak restaurant where we dined on sirloin. Barney joined us as we were rummaging around, and then a scroungy female who went by Britney. The skanky bitch was in heat and soon there were toms all around, some I'd never seen before. I left Homer went to get in line. Never pass up pussy was my motto.

"Barney's balls were long gone, so he was locked in exclusively on the steak leftovers. A couple of kitchen workers came out and stood on the steps smoking and talking and idly watching us. 'Hey man,' one of them said to Homer. 'Don't be doing that.' He disappeared into the kitchen and returned with a large platter. Homer climbed out of the dumpster and mounted the two stairs to the kitchen stoop and took it from the guy's hand, thanking him profusely. On it was a slightly overcooked porterhouse someone had sent back to the kitchen along with two baked potatoes and some veggies. 'Leave the plate and utensils on the stoop when you're finished,' the guy said.

"I was happy for Homer. We visited the steak place several times a week, and on each trip the kitchen help fed him. They also gave him cigarettes and occasionally a couple of bucks to buy wine. It was like adoption, and Homer was always polite and respectful and made sure the guys knew how grateful he was.

"Wherever we dined Homer walked around the corner afterward to one of the streets and panhandled. When he'd collected enough for a couple of bottles of cheap wine and a pack of smokes it was back to the alley to hang out with us cats. We didn't do any actual talking at first. Winter set in and the nights were getting chilly even though this is Florida. Homer started hitting the trash bins along the streets for heavier clothes and stashed them behind the car seat. I hadn't noticed until then, but also stashed back there was a battered old satchel filled with papers. He began carrying it with him everywhere and collecting discarded manuscripts from the dumpster behind the university dorm. He kept sheets of paper that weren't soaked in pizza grease and blank on one or both sides. He also kept ballpoint pens he found. Then after panhandling and buying the night's wine and cigs he sat underneath a street lamp and wrote, propping the satchel against his knees as a makeshift desk. I didn't pay attention to what he was writing—meaning I never sat on his satchel—just that he wrote obsessively.

"The weeks passed and Homer's behavior became erratic and unpredictable. He drank more and we started frequenting dumpsters behind bars. These seldom held anything edible, but occasionally there was a discarded liquor bottle with a swallow left in the bottom. Homer drank everything. When his income from panhandling picked up during winter tourist season he could afford to buy whiskey and a joint now and then to smooth over the wine's aftertaste. And we started to talk. His life was shot, he said. Over. Finished. His girlfriend had kicked him to the curb before he became homeless, declaring him a loser, a lounger, and possibly a fag, but at the very least a mediocre scholar.

"At the time he'd set out to prove her wrong and began going around with the cuffs of his long-sleeved shirts rolled up two turns on his forearms, the right number equaling cool. He affected stern expressions for benefit of his students, who weren't fooled and hooted at him behind his back. They once caught him picking his nose during a contemplative moment, filmed it with a smartphone, and posted the video on YouTube where it accumulated a million hits; in total, he calculated, 173.61 consecutive twenty-four days—*nearly six fucking months*—during which a million bored yahoos wasted fifteen seconds of their lives picking their own noses and sucking air while watching him picking his.

"A man of genuine profoundness might have been spared that humiliation. He lurched through life stepping on his shadow, unable to dissociate himself from the stilted image he believed his true self should emulate, eventually becoming a shell. He neglected his appearance; he had no income and his landlord evicted him. He took to drinking cheap wine and sleeping on sidewalks until finding the abandoned car. His only friends and comrades became his cats, and he felt a leaden guilt for having assigned them numbers instead of names before realizing there was no difference, that both are merely denotations. And numbers offered the added advantage of masking our identities from government spies who no doubt had been monitoring his research. Once the structure of stray cat societies had been deciphered, direct extrapolation of the data to human societies by the military-industrial complex was sure to follow. Nothing would be the same. Homer desperately feared exclusion from the apocalypse, the possibility of the world ending without him.

"There was also something else. Homer dropped clumsily to the sidewalk and started to weep, hair and beard a tangled shrub of greasy keratin lubricated with salty tears. He swallowed a sob and blew snot into his moustache. He said that Barry Hannah once wrote, 'You should not name something more elegant then you. . .' Homer interpreted this to mean us, his scroungy, unreliable, indifferent research subjects whom he'd assigned numbers of one to a hundred. We were his standard of elegance.

"Before abandoning the university completely, Homer printed a hard copy of his unfinished dissertation and was using the blank reverse sides of the pages to write an epic poem. The manuscript and field notes on our movements, diet, general behavior, and mating habits totaled more than four hundred pages, plenty of paper to expend on verses penned under the street lamp, and he was collecting more all the time. Who knew how long his poem would be? No matter. Art, he said, had no beginning and no end. It represented the expression of a life lived along a continuum. Art was a dynamic, shape-shifting wraith, a tenuous link between reality and the imagination. I understood none of this, but Homer's eloquence and excitement were infectious. He once said to me, 'I've found my ecological niche, #77, and you're the first to know. I'm converting my field notes taken on you cats into iambic pentameter. The result will revolutionize the arts. I'll be hailed as a new Whitman. Please spread the word to the rest of our research group.' Meaning the neighborhood cats, of course. With that he returned to scribbling under the street lamp.

"This basic routine continued into the following summer, with Homer now shouting invectives at strangers, mumbling to himself, and carrying out increasingly irrational conversations with me. He became even smellier and more disheveled. At some point he lost or discarded his flip-flops and was now barefoot and unkempt in every way, his clothes literally falling from him in rotten chunks like the dead epidermis of a molting elephant seal. The nails of his fingers and toes had lengthened into yellowed claws and he was starting to lose teeth. Barney dropped by the abandoned car occasionally, but he wasn't interested in people now that a despicable representative of humankind had cut off his cojones. Other cats simply came and went, appearing and vanishing like specters.

"As I've said before, we cats aren't sociable, although I felt a vague twinge of responsibility for Homer that to this day I can't explain. He was a benighted and aleatory soul, but generous. An example of this last is when we rummaged in that dumpster behind the university dorm for remains of pizzas; he always gave me any anchovies or slices of pepperoni, knowing cats are carnivorous and unable to subsist on vegetables and carbohydrates. This did not go unappreciated, and I say it while recognizing that few animals measure up to cats for being self-centered and narcissistic.

"Homer's sensory perception had faded noticeably since we started hanging out. Nose hairs glued together with boogers occluded his nostrils; his ear holes were stuffed with wax-impregnated hairs. The thick glasses he wore when we first met had long since been lost. He could neither smell nor hear, and he reported that he saw the world through eyeballs seemingly smeared with Vaseline. As a result of this extreme myopia he could read the fine print on the label of a gin bottle but any large moving object in the distance had an equal chance of being a city bus or runaway hippopotamus. But he saw enough. Once while staring intently at a rain puddle he said, 'I know you're color-blind #77, but I have to tell you, there's nothing more beautiful than slanting sunlight reflecting off a gasoline spill. The spectrum! The iridescence!'

"Something had to give. I could sense an adumbration still too vague to identify. Keep in mind how limited my experience with humans was back then. I didn't consider them evil or especially calumnious beings, although that was about to change. As a database of human behavior, I had only Barney's experiences and my own narrow escape from the so-called cat lovers.

"Then one fall morning the police crept up to our car and dragged Homer out. I was about to make a run for it until a pair of hands grabbed me too. I fought and bit and scratched but the hands were protected by heavy gloves. I was shoved into a carrying cage and put in the back of a van. It was the same group of do-gooders once again out to save us strays from ourselves and take away our freedom.

"Homer was fighting too. '*I won't go quietly you peckerwoods!*' he shouted. '*There is no Heaven or Hell, just people standing shoulder-to-shoulder up to their chins in shit while a garbled 8-track plays endlessly at full volume! Listen, can you hear the music? It's Donny and Marie Osmond, and you're going to hear those same songs for eternity, so get used to it!* They had cuffed him and two uniformed officers were trying to cram him into the closest of the two cop cruisers. '*And keep your goddamn hands off my poetry!*' Homer yelled.

"One of the cops—there were four—had opened Homer's satchel on the car hood and pulled out some papers. 'Hey, listen to this,' he said. 'Every page has nothing but FUCK FUCK FUCK FUCK FUCK FUCK written on it. There's at least a couple of reams of this shit, just FUCK written in pen from top to bottom of every page, over and over.' The fourth cop was leaning against the driver's door, chewing a toothpick. He brushed some donut crumbs off his distended belly and looked at the ground, maybe hoping for a glimpse of his feet. 'Jesus, this fucker stinks,' he said. 'The garage guys are gonna have to powerwash our cruiser. Jesus, what a stink. Well we got him off the streets. Let's get his pathetic ass to the mental ward. Jesus, he stinks.' That's the last time I saw Homer."

"So what became of you?" I said, topping off my snifter and lighting a cigar.

"Same as happened to Barney. They took me to a vet who knocked me out with a shot of ketamine, wormed and vaccinated me, killed my fleas and ticks, and sliced off the family jewels. I woke up at an animal shelter in a tiny cage furnished with a bowl of water, another of kibbles, and a litter pan. Days passed. People came and went, mostly caretakers, but also prospective 'adoptive parents, I think they were called by the staff. I was sandwiched between two other strays in separate cages. We couldn't see each other, although we could communicate. They'd been caught in live-traps baited with canned cat food. None of us had much to say. The situation was too depressing. Now we were 'rescue cats,' a term that makes my ass ache. I mourned for myself and for Homer, also incarcerated somewhere and raving, hopefully with his nuts intact. I mourned for my own departed testicles and for my pecker, which would never again penetrate and torment a female in heat with its tiny spines.

"Eventually I was 'adopted' by a middle-aged couple living on the fourth floor of a high-rise. I had run of the apartment, but eventually went berserk anyway. I ripped up the furniture, climbed the curtains, and took to pissing on the carpets. Of course I knew better, but with escape impossible this was my only way out. Sure enough I was 'unadopted' and wound up in that community cage at Cat Depot. Christ, I must have been there several months before you and Lucia came along. By then I was ready for anything."

"You could run away again," I said. "We don't monitor your comings and goings."

"Naw, I've come to like it here. You can tell because I don't piss on the rugs. Of course, you have mostly tile floors, but still. . . And I've learned lots from those books you've been writing, except the one about wolves and dogs. I found that pretty boring, not to mention unnecessary. In my opinion, all canids should be gassed. The world would be a better place."

"No doubt they'd feel the same about you," I said.

"I'm surprised you still picked me, having suspected my trashy past during our interview," Jinx said.

"I suppose if we'd wanted a posh, pampered, pusillanimous pussy we'd have looked elsewhere, like at a pet store or in the classifieds. And we'd have picked out a cute fluffy little kitten, not a grown alley cat with a bad attitude. What a shame there aren't charm schools for cats like there are for dogs."

"That's because dogs so desperately need them. Anyhow it sounds like another kind of jail sentence. I'd just run away and go back to the streets where life is a smorgasbord."

I said, "I hope street food still suits your palate because that's all you'll be enjoying if you run away from here. Keep in mind you're not a tomcat any longer; you have no balls. You've been detesticularized. Hey, what a great word! I'm adding it to my vocabulary."

"Very funny," said Jinx. "You can't know how much I miss my offspring; that is, if I could find them." I glanced his way and thought I saw the wisp of a grin, but a cat's lips are rigidly fixed, as I've said before, and incapable of subtlety. He's only a cat, my brain told itself, forgetting momentarily that Jinx could hear this internal monologue. The trick was not to think in his presence. This might take practice. I let my brain shift around enough mental furniture to make room for a pregnant pause, but that space vanished immediately. So much for not thinking. Whatever a "pregnant pause" might mean, it was distracting as all hell. Could it be a pause distinguished by a metaphorical protuberance of the abdomen? The apparition of a gestating hiatus? Delayed implantation of an embryo onto the uterine wall, as practiced by certain species of seals? Who cared? If the intention was to quit thinking, then more dope and alcohol ought to help. I lit another joint and took a hit. I topped off the snifter of rum.

I was still flying high as if I could actually achieve lift by flapping my arms. The preliminary aerodynamics seemed straightforward from the equations I'd seen. Maybe I should learn to glide as an evolutionary first step. I could climb onto the railing and dive headfirst off the deck.

"Don't do it," Jinx said. "I hear what you're thinking. You'll break your ass and probably your neck. A cat would land on its feet from one storey up, but a human? Not a chance. And you better keep an eye on that cigar ash. Looks like it's getting pretty long."

Okay, I thought, that's good advice about the flying. I leaned back in my chair. "Shows how much you know, smart guy," I said. "Has a cat ever smoked a cigar? Ha! I doubt it very much. Thing is you let the ash accumulate purposely because it cools the smoke being drawn into your mouth. Watch."

With an exaggerated movement to make my point I drew on the cigar satisfied to see the end glow red. Instantly the hot ash fell directly on my bare scrotum. I'd discarded the hospital gown, which now lay in a heap beside the chair, and was sitting there naked. Suddenly there was intense pain and a scent of burning pubic hair. I jumped to my feet and started hopping around batting at my lower parts to flick off the ashes, stubbing my toe against the bottom railing. *Ouch, ouch! Jesus fucking Christ that hurts, and now my toe! Oh shit, oh dear god!* What Norman Mailer wrote in *Ancient Evenings* is surely true: 'If pain is a fundament, then a blade of grass can know all there is.' Not just a blade of grass; a scrotum too, and a toe. But nobody dies of such injuries. Like any geezer I had to keep morbid thoughts at bay. The burn and my toe would heal, the pubes would grow back. Don't think about it, I thought. This was Florida, where we're all slowly humping like inchworms toward the crematorium.

Cats can't laugh as humans do but I could sense Jinx telepathically making a try. At least he didn't sneeze and go into convulsions this time. "You're such a pussy," he said.

Those words set me off. "*I've taken your shit long enough! I'm a pussy?*" I shouted. "*Me? No fucking way I'm a pussy, you. . .you goddamn pussy!*"

Hearing the commotion the dog next door started barking. The neighbors had let it outside to take a leak. Then I heard Frank say through the shrubbery, "Steve is that you? What in hell's going on? Who's a pussy?"

"Jinx is a pussy," I said. "He's nothing but a fucking pussy."

"Uh, Steve, isn't Jinx your cat?" said Frank.

"Right, he's a cat. He's sitting here in the other chair claiming I'm the pussy, not him. He's pissing me off."

"So you're having this loud conversation with a cat? Are you drunk or stoned?"

"Yes," I said.

"I'll be over right after I let the dog inside. Is your door unlocked?"

"I don't remember, but come through it anyway."

A few minutes later Frank showed up carrying a bottle of wine, permitting me to deduce that most likely the door had been unlocked. He first went to the kitchen to uncork the bottle and get a glass, then stepped onto the deck. There were only two chairs, but it was dark now, and Jinx relinquished his to go ratting out in the dunes.

"Jesus Christ, you're naked," Frank said, taking a sip from his glass and then lighting a cigar. "Did I ever mention your cat shits in my front yard every morning?"

"Many times," I said. "And you're very observant: I'm indeed naked, and I also just burned the hell out of my scrotum with a cigar ash. Wouldn't you yelp if that happened?"

"I certainly would, but with a little more dignity. Then again I don't ordinarily smoke cigars while naked. I like to keep my testicles covered."

I said, "Okay but that's still no reason to call a guy a pussy, like Jinx did. He's never smoked a cigar and remains unaware of the instantaneous hurt they can cause. Insulting me during such a moment of distress is evidence of an insensate disposition."

"Ummm," Frank said. "What's that on the floor?"

"Hospital gown. I just got sprung from Sarasota Memorial a few hours ago, I think. Probably before you came over. Have you been here long? Gall bladder extraction surgery. They stuffed me with lots of good drugs and I've been trying to keep the buzz going."

"You seem to have succeeded," Frank said. "I'm jealous except for the scorched scrotum part. Who needs a gall bladder anyway? Isn't it basically a grease trap? And say, don't bogart that doobie."

Printed in Great Britain
by Amazon